THE BIRTH OF TITCHFIELD
and other stories

Tales inspired by Titchfield's Past

edited by John Hiett

THE BIRTH OF TITCHFIELD AND OTHER STORIES

Published by Magic Flute Publications 2018

ISBN 978-1-909054-50-9

Magic Flute Publications is an imprint of

Magic Flute Artworks Limited

231 Swanwick Lane

Southampton SO31 7GT

www.magicfluteartworks.com

A catalogue description of this book is available from the British Library

Contents

Preface

This collection of short stories sprang from an idea that Titchfield's long and rich history could be revealed through fictional treatment. Several writers were approached and each contributed a story or two, The authors have taken an historical event as their starting point and used their imagination and creativity to add colour to the story. These are, of course, works of fiction, and anyone wishing to learn more about the evnt should follow up on those already published books of Tichfield history.

The stories cover a long period - from the Dark Ages to the 1950s.

I would like to thank the writers - Shirley Bethell, Lois Bird, Lorraine Davies,Taliesin Driver, Hannah Hiett, Peter Hiett, Rosa Johnson, Margaret Pace and Margaret Thompson for their excellent contributions. Thanks also to Ann Wheal and Bryan Dunleavy for their editorial assistance, and Bryan Dunleavy for designing the book and the cover.

John Hiett
September 2018

516 AD

The Birth of Titchfield

The Birth of Titchfield

Taliesin Driver

Trudging through the forest, keeping close to the river, heading down stream. The ruts on the floor of the forest were frozen solid. Millions of bright stars cast shadows through the bare trees. Cold hungry animals moved nearby.

The boy Swithun, already a man at fourteen, carried his father's satchel of tools. The man was half carrying his wife. But she could go no further.

"It is too late. The baby is coming now." She lay on the ground and the man covered her with his coat. The boy hunted for dry twigs to start a fire and grudgingly the flames began.

The woman was old. This was her fifth child. Only Swithun, her first born, had survived infancy. The baby was born yelling. Swithun saw it had no eyebrows or knee caps. Its fingers were pink, its body purple. It was covered with streaks of mess and blood. The woman had given up the ghost.

The man covered her decently and put the baby to her dead breast. Snow began to fall. The first flakes stuck to each other. Then it whirled about them in big furry flakes.

All sound stopped. The boy hurried to find more dry wood and built up the fire. Man and boy watched as the snow formed a blanket over the woman and child. It was somehow comforting, as if the blanket was warm.

They waited till dawn, then set off again.

They walked south , following the river. It looked black and uninviting, like something evil. The events of the previous day filled their minds. Hunger was knawing away at them. So they walked unaware into a clearing where four men awaited them. They had blonde hair and beards. They were Saxons. The Saxons had been settled on the south coast for a generation now, and no-one was concerned to force them away. For the most part they kept to themselves, with occasional forays into British territory.

These four were not settlers, but renegades, unwanted by even their own people. The father spoke to the boy in the old language, "Swithun, these men will kill us both. Run away into the forest. Save yourself. But come back when you're ready and deal with them."

Swithun disappeared into the trees while his father fought the four men. It didn't last long.

Swithun had lived amongst trees all his life. He knew how to move silently. He knew how to live off the land. He took his knife from his belt and sharpened it on a stone. He found some worms under a pile of leaves, squeezed the dirt out of them with his fingers and ate them raw. He found a Hawthorn tree. The small red berries, amongst the dark green leaves and big thorns, grew in profusion. The berries were small and the stones within were large, but there was enough flesh around the stone to stave off his hunger pains. Then he was ready.

His father had taught him "Go in peace. Help other people when you can, and they will help you when they can. But if any man does you harm, make sure that he is not given the chance to hurt you a second time."

In this thought Swithun was implacable.

He saw the fox looking at him. It was red, with golden eyes, and unafraid. Its whiskers swept back along its slim snout. It walked a little way away, turned its head and looked back at him. Swithun walked towards it, and the fox led the way again. Near the end of the day he heard the Saxons. They were having a good time, drinking wine and discussing how much money they would get for the tools and clothes of Swithun's father.

In an hour or so one of the men moved a couple of hundred yards into the trees to open his bowels. Swithun crept silently behind him, and as he squatted with his breeks around his ankles, caught him by the hair in one hand and had his knife to his throat. "You know who I am, don't you?" he said and before the man could answer slit his throat. He sat him down in his own mess his blood steaming as it hit the snow.

"Two piles of ordure" he thought.

He kept his distance for the next few days, he and the fox. There seemed to be a bond between them. Sometimes Swithun would think that this fox looked at him like his father used to look at him, with tenderness and pride. The fox brought birds to him, which he would wrap in clay and bake in the fire. When cooked, the feathers came away with the clay. One morning the fox led him to a hillside, and Swithun saw a cleft in the hill, near an overgrown clearing. Inside the cleft he found a hovel lined with wood, covered in grass, with a hole through the grass above a hearth. Someone had lived here years ago, and cleared the ground to plant crops. The door had rotted away, but inside was a bench and a few implements including a rusty but wicked animal trap, big enough to catch a bear.

He cleaned it up, greased it and sharpened the teeth. It took a long time, but at last it was working freely.

He knew that the Saxons would be hunting him, and he wanted to lead them to him. He lit a fire in the hearth, and put on enough damp wood for smoke to rise through the hole in the turf roof.

When the fox came to him he knew that the Saxons were nearby. He coated the teeth with deadly nightshade. He set the trap under leaves at the entrance to the hovel, banked up the fire and left to watch from a distance.

The three Saxons came carefully. They watched for a long time. One went behind the hovel in case there was a rear exit. The other two rushed for the doorway. One went through brandishing his staff, the other stepped on the trap which closed on his leg and almost severed it. He wouldn't survive that wound. Two down, two to go.

The coming of spring made life easier for him. Hedgehogs appeared from hibernation. They tasted like chicken when he wrapped it in clay and baked it on a fire. More birds appeared. Swithun walked with his pockets full of pebbles, and he became skilled at throwing the pebbles at them. There were swarms of sparrows, and he could hardly miss.

New growth appeared on the forest floor. He picked some strange looking mushrooms which he cooked in a cauldron he had found in the hovel.

The mushrooms tasted fine, but after he ate he fell to the ground and had a vision. He thought he heard the sound of thundering hooves, and out of the mist appeared a magnificent white bull, with a man in crimson on it's back. The pair careered around in front of him, before the man leaned forward and cut the throat of the bull. Around them ran a dog, while a serpent, a raven and a scorpion waited for the bull's blood.

The Saxons were still hunting him; he knew that they were near when the fox barked. He put more mushrooms in the pot, built up the fire and slipped away. The two Saxons came to his fire by different directions. "He is near" one said, "We'll run him down."

So confident were they that two grown men could run down a mere boy that they took time to eat the mushrooms before setting off. He watched as they ate, and they fell to the forest floor.

Soon one awoke, and looking at the other saw horns growing from his head. He lashed out at the horns with his staff, but no matter how often he struck them, the horns continued to grow.

"Three down, one to go" thought Swithun. The last Saxon, driven by terror, saw beasts all around him. A monstrous wolf appeared. He ran wildly, filling his pockets with stones to throw at the beasts pursuing him. He ran downhill until he came to the river, swollen with spring rains. He leapt in, and, weighed down with the stones in his pocket, sank to the bottom.

"Amen" said Swithun.

The old man was seated outside a cave, on a patch of grass. A spring came out of the rock behind him and formed a pool in the grass before trickling over the edge and down the hill. Not far away was a river – the old man called it the Meon, and just beyond that a settlement. It was no more than eight dwellings, perhaps 40 souls. Its very smallness probably kept it safe from Saxon raiders. It wasn't worth the risk for such small reward.

"Ah, Swithun" said the old man, "I've been waiting for you."

"How did you know my name, and how did you know I was coming? I didn't know myself until I arrived here."

"It was ordained. My name is Emrys. Some call me an enchanter, others a healer, that I have the sight, that I am a magician. But I am an old man, and before I go I will pass on my knowledge to an apprentice. That apprentice is you, Swithun."

The cave was spacious. Towards the rear was a hearth. The smoke was drawn into a crack in the roof, a natural chimney. There was furniture, a large chest full of rolled up books, and a harp.

Emrys moved to the chest and unrolled a book. "Here is my book of healing. I will teach you to read, and then you will learn of the plants I gather, and the potions and poultices and pastes I make, and the ailments they can treat."

"This book is my song book, that one on the great happenings of the past. When you have learned all this you will be able to foretell the future more easily."

"I have visions, but I cannot call on them just when I want them. I have to wait for the gods to decide what I should see in the flames of my fire. But I can make fire without a flint, and I will teach you how to do that."

The boy nodded.

"Your father taught you well, to live in peace but to avenge wrongs done to you. I will teach you more. You are not a soldier. You will not always be able to defend yourself by force. I will teach you the dark arts. You should live in peace with your fellow man. But people will soon learn that any man who is malevolent towards you will suffer. They will be dogged by illness and accident and bad luck. Their crops will rot in the ground. Their wives will be barren. I will teach you how to bring this about, and I know you will use this power wisely."

"I will teach you Latin and Greek because when you travel the world you will find these tongues useful."

"In two years I will have taught you all that I know, and then you will travel to distant parts. You will go to Rome and Athens. You will cross the sea into Africa and learn wondrous things. When you return I will be awaiting you. And then I will leave you."

Swithun stayed with Emrys for two years. He remembered all he was told or read. He built his own harp and wrote his own songs.

At 16 he crossed the narrow sea to Less Britain and journeyed South through France. He saw great cathedrals being built. He learned to speak French. He earned a living as a jongleur, and as a healer. He travelled to Rome, to Greece, the cradle of democracy, to Constantinople, where East meets West, and then to Alexandria, the home of Ptolemy's library.

Ptolemy had been dead for three centuries, but his library remained. He was Egyptian, but wrote in Greek. He had written on astronomy (he could forecast eclipses of the Sun) on astrology, geography (his map of Britain was recognisable), on optics (including refraction, reflection and colours), and on the mathematics of music and harmony. He and successive librarians gathered together the works of other scholars to form the greatest collection of knowledge in the world.

Swithun stayed there for two years, absorbing all this information, and then made his way home by a different route. He was 23 years of age.

"Tell me everything" said Emrys. The old man and the young one sat companionably by the hearth and talked for three days. Swithun recalled everything he had seen, and the old man lived those travels through Swithun's eyes. When he had finished Emrys said, "I am well pleased with you. You are no longer my apprentice; I am your student. You will do great things and I must go to the place I have prepared for myself."

Swithun set out on his quest. He travelled through forests and across meadows and met no-one until he came to a great castle on a hill.

He spoke to a man working in a field. "Who lives in yonder castle?" he asked. "Why, that is our master, the Earl Tidic" was the reply. Swithun ventured to pay homage to Tidic, and was kindly received by him.

"What manner of man are you?" asked Tidic.

"If it please you Lord, I am a soothsayer and a bard. I have travelled to many lands, learned many tongues. I have seen monuments to kings of Egypt that stand many times taller than the tallest tree. I have seen oceans made of sand. I have dined with the Empress of Constantinople. I have seen strange

9

animals, bigger than horses, ridden by men into the waterless desert. I have studied in Rome and Greece and Egypt."

"Know you, soothsayer. My men tell me of a monster nearby in the forest. It is a stag, swifter than any bird. It has a horn in the centre of its forehead as long as a man's arm. It eats from the top of trees and kills every animal it finds. Those it doesn't kill die from hunger. And every night it drains the fish ponds so that the fish die. What should I do about that?"

"Lord, in that forest, too, live the old people. They speak the old tongues. They worship the old Gods, they practice magic. Beware of hurting the beast that protects them."

"Those old people have wedded each other for so long that they are sickly and few in number. I have ten thousand fighting men. How can they harm me?"

"There will be a sign, Lord. In two days time, in the middle of the day, the sun will disappear for a short time. Darkness will lie upon the land. Then the sun will appear again. This is the sign you should note."

As Swithun predicted, the sun was eclipsed, and although Tidic was impressed he was not a man to be frightened. Urged on by his 14 sons, he determined to challenge the beast. He dressed in his armour and, with a dog to raise the beast, rode into the forest on his palfrey. The stag ran at him, but he had his horse step aside, and as the stag passed him he swung his sword and cut off its head with one blow. Thus he came to be known as Tidic the Mighty.

His palace was near Wickham, where the old Roman road from Winchester met the road between Chichester and Bitterne. He had nine captains of war bands and above these captains was Owein Mighty Grasp.

He planned a banquet at this palace to celebrate his victory. He invited all nobles of the Dominium to a feast which was to last for three days. He commanded Swithun to compose a song of praise to him and to sing it to his guests on the first day of the banquet.

Swithun took his leave. He gathered mushrooms and ate them. He fell into a dreamworld, and when he awoke the song was already in his mind. When the banquet was ready he took his harp to the dining hall and sang a paeon of praise. He praised Tidic's mighty shoulders, his mighty courage and his mighty loins. He told the story of Tidic's conquest of the monstrous stag. But he also prayed for the protection of Tidic by the Gods Castor and Pollux, twin sons of Leda. Tidic was angered by this and told Swithun he would not pay him for the song.

A servant came to Swithun and told him that two young men awaited him outside. He left the hall to meet them. As he talked to them the ground began to tremble. A rumble started beneath their feet and rocks fell down the hillside. Behind them the banqueting hall shook, and they watched as the roof fell in with a thundering crash. Clouds of dust arose in the bright sunlight, and as it settled the devastation became clear. The whole building was flat, and all sixty people within perished.

Swithun addressed the sons of the dead nobles. "This is what must be done. I must go into the forest and talk to the old people. While I am away you must uncover the bodies. You will not recognise them, but I remember where everyone was sitting." He drew a plan of the banqueting hall and marked the seating places. "Here at the main table sat Tidic, and to his left was Taliesin, chief of bards. On Tidic's right was Arwal Hengist, Wiht Horsa, Finn Getwolf, Wipped Oslac and Stuf Wiht. Next to Taliesin was Ethelbert Aese, Port Biede, Woden Octa and Gweir Big-Breadth."

Swithun went through the whole banqueting hall, naming the people there. He told them that they must arrange the bodies with as much dignity as they could, each in his own coffin, and cover the bodies with honey, which would preserve them.

He went into the forest, bearing on his sleeve the emblem which showed he was a messenger, and which would allow no-one to attack him. He did not see anyone until suddenly he was surrounded by small dark men. He greeted them in the old language. "I come in peace."

The old people were pagans. They worshipped pagan gods. They had a shrine to Myrddin, and were governed by druids. They wanted only to be left alone, to live their lives in their own way.

The druids would neither deny nor confirm that they were responsible for the earthquake. "Come back in one year," they said, "and if we have been unmolested in that time, we will either confirm or deny it."

He reached agreement with them and returned to the palace, where he gathered the nobles about him. Tidic's eldest son had a hump back, so his second son, Ticce, had slain him and taken control.

"Counsellor" he said, "tell us what we are to do."

Swithun told them that he had seen the future. They were to prepare a barrow to his design, in a place chosen by him, close to Emrys' cave. The barrow would never be found because he would build it underground. He set men to dig two tunnels into the hillside, sloping upwards, and near the end sloping more steeply. The excavated soil was easily removed from the tunnel on sledges because the loaded sledges were pulled downhill, and the empty ones pulled uphill. The tunnels were supported by posts on either side. When the tunnels broke through into the air on the other side of the hill natural ventilation took fresh air through the two tunnels. They then dug a third tunnel between them.

A cloth door was placed just above the cross tunnel in the first long tunnel, and just below the cross tunnel in the second tunnel. In this way fresh air was directed up the first tunnel, along the cross tunnel and up the second tunnel to the exit. In that cross tunnel, the workers made a burial chamber to Swithun's design.

While this work was going on, Swithun searched for the great treasure buried by the Romans before they left. He put himself into the mind of the Roman general, and decided that it was buried either at Oxford or at Amesbury, where the giant stones stood. He went first to Amesbury, with one of the war bands led by Owein Mighty Grasp, and a train of mules. He walked amongst the stones. He noted the position of the grave of an old king. He consulted the stars, and then he knew where the treasure was buried.

They took it home, and in a great ceremony placed the coffins in the burial chamber, in the order they had been in the banqueting hall, and surrounded them with the Roman Treasure. They removed the posts from the two main tunnels and allowed them to collapse. The surface subsided a little, but nothing was visible at ground level. Only the red kites flying above could see the faint parallel lines of the old tunnels.

They made shrines at the old entrances, one to the god Myrddin, and one to Cybele, Roman goddess of protection.

Swithun placed three enormous stones carefully in position. "These are Sarsen stones" he said, "perhaps in a thousand years' time some astronomer will, by studying the stars and the position of these stones, find Tidic's barrow. But it is more likely that before those times the stones will have been moved, and the burial place lost forever."

Swithun returned to live in Emrys' cave. Ticce was a good ruler. He protected the old people in the forest, and the hamlet near Swithun's cave, which he named Ticcefeld. Untroubled by Saxons the people prospered. There was plenty of game in the forest, deer and boars and rabbits, and fish in the river. They grew their crops in the fields and built storehouses to tide them over poor times.

Swithun travelled. He went to Hadrian's Wall and saw the remains of the huge forts built every mile along its length, and the temples of Mithras. He went to Cornwall and paid homage to the King there.

He went to Caer Llion on Usk. He went to Winchester and built a home there for scholars. His ambition was to develop a library there to rival that of Ptolemy. He was revered throughout the land. There was not a man in Britain more mighty in counsel than he.

At his cave in Ticcefeld he studied plants and animals and insects and drew diagrams of them until his eyes began to fail. From his cave he could keep an eye of Tidic's barrow and on Ticcefeld. The miller brought him bread, and people brought him meat and fish. In return he attended to their ills.

As he grew into an old man he gave instruction that on his death he was to be left in his cave with his books and his harp, and the entrance collapsed. He said that if any man ever entered Tidic's barrow his spirit would rise from the cave through the ventilation crevice, and he would make the tomb raider suffer.

So revered was Swithun that even after his death fathers named their sons after him.

The name of the boy in the forest lives on. Tidic's barrow remains safe in his care. And Ticcefeld too survives.

680 AD

The Vicar's Daughter

The Vicar's Daughter

Lois Bird

It was a cold night for the time of year. It was nearly spring. The first flowers should have been opening, but instead a frost lay thick on the ground. A young man by the name of Willum, approaching his 21st birthday, walked along the street, huddled against the cold and hurrying to his warm home, where his mother would have lit the fire and his father would be waiting for his supper. As Willum entered his house he felt the heat of the fire and the smell of the welcoming rabbit stew. The cold night was wiped instantly from his mind. His father embraced him in welcome. On any other night this would have been very out of the ordinary, but tonight was special for Willum and his family. The air was full of a dangerous happiness as they gathered around the table.

Although extremely handsome, Willum was unusually tall with bright blonde hair, which made him stick out in their community. He had been born here in Titchfield, as had his parents, but his decedents came from far to the north, across the sea. They were of the Meonwara tribe, but Willum's family worshipped the old gods of the Norsemen. The father of these gods was known as Odin, and he was fearsome indeed, but it was the goddess Hel who really struck fear in their hearts. It was to Hel that Willum and his father now raised their drinks in offering, calling her name as they did so.

"Quiet" hissed his normally gentle mother, in a strangled tone. "They'll hear!".

Willum looked at his mother, still beautiful at forty-three although a little wrinkled. He saw the fear in her eyes as she glanced out of the window, peering into the dark street as if expecting the bishop of Oxford himself to come charging into their hut and arrest them all for their paganism. This fear had been following her for as long as Willum could remember. He was sure that it was the cause of her premature grey hair. Wilfred's conversion of Willum's tribe had been going on for several decades now. Pagans across the kingdoms had been facing persecution for nearly one hundred years. Even before Wilfrid's focus on the Meonwara, the Saxons had been killing them off one by one, just for being different. These were uncertain times indeed, and it was not safe to turn openly against Christianity.

Across the town, in a small but pleasant cottage near where the new church would be, a beautiful young woman, only in her seventeenth year, sat at her own table, with her own family, completing her own religious observances.

'Our Father, who art in Heaven", her father, Edgar, began, "Hallowed be thy name".

Edith stared absentmindedly out of the window with her big dark eyes as the priest continued with the Lord's Prayer. She wondered if this new town Titchfield would hold any interest for her. She had left good friends behind her from their previous posting, and she missed them terribly already. But her father had to go where he was needed, and the bishop of Winchester, Hædde, had asked for him specifically to oversee the construction of the new Minster Church there, and to become the area's only priest. It would be a difficult job, her father had told her, for all of them, but the Lord's work had to be done. Sweeping her brown hair away from her face, she brought herself back to her father, just in time for the end of the prayer.

"For thine is the kingdom the power and the glory, forever and ever, Amen"

"Amen" Edith and her mother chorused.

During dinner, Edith's father explained in more detail about how the church would be built and the expected timescale for it.

"The building of the church is only the beginning of course. Our excellent Bishop Hædde has trusted me with the great task of tending to the entire area. There will be a great many non-believers and pagans in the corners of the community. I expect a great deal more who hide in plain sight, pretending to have converted to the light but who still practise their dark ways in the secrecy of their own homes. These will be the most difficult to help, dear daughter, but help them we must. It is our duty, not as members of the clergy, but as good Christians, to bring them into our fold. Can I rely on your help in this matter?"

Edith did not hesitate in her rely of "Of course, father, it is not only my duty but my pleasure to help you with the ways of the Church". Inside, however, in the privacy of her mind, her answer was somewhat different. She knew that she wanted more than this life, more than being a dutiful daughter, and someday a dutiful wife, but she also knew that girls like her did not get to make those sorts of decisions. However, more than that, she didn't think she agreed with her Father's insistence on converting every pagan they found. These people were members of the community as much as they were, and as long as it didn't hurt anybody, did it really matter who they prayed to? These were Edith's private musings, she knew she could never voice them to her parents.

The next day, Edith walked into the town, lovely and warm in her thick coat with its fur lined hood. Although Edith had intended on some exploring, she was soon tempted by the wonderful smell coming from the bakery. The warming smell of freshly baked bread had always held a special power over her, and she made her way immediately into the shop. Edith took her time admiring and choosing her loaf, having a very pleasant conversation with the baker's wife as she did so, before eventually choosing a small but perfectly round one. She was sure her parents would like it. Just to be safe, she bought two. Leaving the bakery, she saw a young woman, about her age, sheltering under a tree in the central green. Curious, Edith went over to investigate. Her father had always said her inquisitive mind would one day land her in trouble, but Edith had never paid much attention.

By some coincidence, the young woman had exactly the same name as the Priest's daughter, but was known simply as Ede. That however was where the similarities ended. Ede was not just poor, she was homeless, finding shelter from the cold and living off scraps and the generosity of the villagers. Ede was a plain girl, and her circumstances had not been kind to her looks. She had matted straggly hair and dull eyes and skin. Despite this, the two became fast friends straight away. Good looks was not something Edith placed much value on, a pure spirit being much more important.

The building of the church was to begin immediately and local men from all over the district would be brought in to help. What's more, the local Lord Aelfred's younger son, Aelfric, would also visit to show his family's support. Edith knew that this was very important, both for the Church and for her Father, but she couldn't shake the feeling of unease that had been growing in her since she had been told about Aelfric. She'd heard of the boy before. "I suppose he's a man now", Edith thought. He was known for his cruelty to servants, animals, and pretty much anybody below his station. She had never liked those who saw themselves as better than others. It wasn't Christian, and it wasn't right to treat people, or animals, like they didn't matter.

At last, construction was ready to begin. The workers were gathered around by the priest, thanked for coming, and promised their wages would be delivered at the end of the week. As a symbol of how important this Church would be for the local area, Aelfric was also present, and gave a short speech to the gathered towns-people. "My father, Lord Aelfred, is very grateful to all of you who have come today, to build our new great church. Thank you for all your hard work", he began. Edith, standing to one-side with her mother, thought he looked rather bored up there, as if he'd rather be almost anywhere else. She was quite sure that those were not his own words, but something that had been written for him - short and simple enough for him to remember, but long enough to satisfy the crowds. Edith had met boys like him before, rich and spoilt and believing themselves better than everyone else. She disliked him instantly. After Aelfric's speech, her father set the labourers to work.

It took Willum a moment to realise the others around him had started towards the tools, as he had been standing transfixed for some time, staring at who he believed to be the Vicar's daughter, Edith, across the path. She was the most beautiful woman he had ever seen, with thick, long brown hair arranged neatly to shimmer down her back, and enormous dark eyes that appeared soft and gentle. Willum suspected that she was in fact more fierce and head-strong than her demure appearance would suggest. He saw Aelfric moving towards her, and beginning a conversation that she was clearly uncomfortable having. For a wild moment, he felt a surge of protective anger that it should be HIMSELF talking to this beautiful girl, not that horrible man with the fake words. The feeling passed as quickly as it had come. "Willum", he scolded himself, "A girl like that will never be with a boy like you, now stop these mad thoughts". Slowly, he turned around, picked up some tools, and followed the other workers.

Since that initial meeting at the church site, Aelfric decided he would make Edith his wife. As the younger son of the local lord, he was used to getting his way. Edith knew that he owned several of his own horses, but he didn't care for them at all. He kicked dogs out of his way, and always carried around his whip to 'get the low-life peasants into shape', as he commented to Edith

21

one time. She'd felt sick after he said that. Edith, who cared for all living things, was disgusted that another human being could be so awful. 'He has a black soul' she thought to herself often. What disgusted her even more, however, was when her father came home one day and told Edith she was to be married.

"It is a fine match" he had said. "A boy of such high station, taking an interest in a lowly priest's daughter! It is quite the honour!"

Edith could see how pleased her father was, but although she was usually such a dutiful daughter, this time she just could not hold her tongue.

"Oh no father, please, do not allow this to happen!" He is such a cruel and horrid man, I just could not bear to be married to such a person."

Her father was shocked, and at first, angry. How his foolish daughter could even think of turning down an offer as splendid as this one, he did not know. She would never make a better match. But after seeing the tears start to fall from his daughter's eyes, a daughter who was not usually prone to hysterics, he began to soften. Not enough, however, to change his mind.

"Daughter" he began, more gently now, "To be married to this boy will not be as bad as you fear. You will come to no harm with him I am sure of it. And as for his behaviour to others, you are right, it is not the Christian way. That, my dear, is where you will be able to bring the change! Coach him in the way of the Lord and he will change how he acts, you shall see".

Edith did not share her father's confidence, but she could see that the discussion was over. With a heavy heart she accepted her fate. She would marry Aelfric.

The weeks went by and the construction continued on the church. Foundations were put into place, and walls were being built. Edith spent a lot of her time at the site, chatting to the workers, and generally helping where she could. When Edith first saw Willum, she was immediately taken with his height and blonde curls - he was the opposite to her in looks and she found it intriguing. Overtime, as they got to know each other, it became apparent that they were also opposites in status. While Willum was always mindful of this, it did not bother Edith at all. They became friends quickly, and, despite Edith's engagement, this soon turned to love.

Willum began to open up to Edith, and as their trust grew, he finally found the courage to reveal his deepest secret, much to his mother's disapproval.

"Edith, I cannot lie to the woman I am falling in love with any longer", Willum said. He was terrified of her reaction but he knew it was the right thing to do.

"My family is of the Meonwara tribe, my ancestors came from across the ocean to the north. It means we worship the Norse Gods. I follow your Christian principles because I believe them to be right, but I do not follow your God. Can you still accept me?"

Edith was startled. She had not expected Willum to say that, he acted like such a good Christian! She knew that it was her duty now to either convert Willum and his family, or to report them. But she knew that she could do neither of those things. She loved him and that was all that mattered now.

"Yes Willum, of course I still accept you. I love you and I will do whatever I can to be with you. I must talk to my father, but I know that I will marry no-one but you".

Edith returned to her parents that night and told them of her choice. They were furious with her. Her mother cried, saying that Aelfric was such a good match and was more than a girl of her status could have ever hoped for. Her father, normally such a gentle man, yelled that she was ruining not just her own reputation but his too. He would not allow it. The priest gave Edith an ultimatum - either she would marry Aelfric, or she would no longer be a part of his family. Her heart breaking into a thousand pieces, Edith tearfully told her parents that she chose

Willum, but she hoped they would come to accept her once more.

In a small town, news spread very quickly. Within days, everyone knew that Edith and Willum were to be married in a pagan ceremony. Aelfric was furious. He had been publicly embarrassed and he was not going to forget it. The night before the wedding, Aelfric confronted Willum in the woods. He wanted his bride back, and he wasn't going to take no for an answer. A fight broke out, and only one person walked away from it.

The sunrise over the woodland barn where Willum and Edith were to be married was beautiful. The soft rays of light that cascaded over the front doors caused the freshly cut grass and the soft blue and pink flowers that lined the path to shimmer angelically. It was a perfect morning. A forager, out early in the day hoping to find his daily catch for the market later that day, paused for a moment to marvel in its beauty. Then he paused some more, staring more closely at the front doors. Squinting through the early morning sun, he took a few steps closer. His eyes widened as he took in the sight in front of him. His mouth opened into a terrible scream that woke up nearly the entire forest, as he stared and stared at Willum's body, fixed crudely to the heavy wooden doors, very clearly dead.

Edith was inconsolable for weeks after Willum's death. She refused to talk to anyone. She stayed shut up in her room. She barely slept and barely ate. Her parents were worried about her health, but secretly, they were glad that Willum was now out of their daughter's life, and that she could stop with all this 'devil worship' as they call it.

One morning, a month after Willum's body was found, Edith left her room to find her parents in the kitchen. She looked oddly calm, her face pale and thin, but her eyes composed. She announced to her parents that Willum's death had been a wake-up call for her, and that she now sees her right path: she will marry Aelfric after all, if he will still take her. Her parents were delighted with this news, and set about immediately composing a letter for the Lord to announce Edith's intentions. They were so pleased that they failed to notice that Edith's eyes were brighter than normal, almost as if she was planning something devious.

Aelfric, of course, still wished to marry Edith He congratulated himself strongly for managing to orchestrate it. The irritating pagan boy was taken care of, he got to marry the most beautiful girl in England, and no one would ever find out what he did. He could not be happier as he arranged the guest list for his wedding, which was to be held as soon as possible. After making such a fuss originally, Edith now said that she wanted it to be the biggest and best wedding in Wessex for a decade, and that it should be unforgettable.

While the wedding preparations were taking place Edith visited her friend from the other side of the river, and she shared her plan.

"Ede, here I've brought you some lovely fresh bread, straight from the bakery"

Ede doesn't reply, but smiles at Edith, her big blue eyes warm and gentle, her only beauty.

"Ede", Edith continues, "I need your help". She goes on to tell Ede everything about Willum, about their love, their engagement, and his murder. She does not cry, there are no tears left, but her eyes flash with anger and deep hatred.

"I will never forgive him, Ede. I will hate him forever but that is not enough. The rest of the world must know who and what he is. His father will always protect him from the law, so my statement must be public, and powerful. That is why I insisted on such a big wedding. I want everyone and anyone gathered around the church when they hear what I have to say"

"Yes Edith, he must pay for his actions" Ede says, "But why have you come to me? How can I help you to do this?"

"I want to secretly swap with you on the morning of the wedding. Aelfric will think it is I walking up the aisle, but instead it will be you under the veil. We are the same height and build after all, it will not be hard. When the veil is removed it will already be over, and be too late. Ede, we share the same name, it will be legal and binding forever. You will be a woman of great means, and Aelfric will be humiliated by being deceived in such a way. This is a lot to ask of you, my friend, but will you do this for me?"

"Dear Edith, you have been my only friend for many years, and have looked after me when I had no-one else to turn to. Of course I shall help you get revenge on this wicked man. And who knows? After we are married, perhaps I can continue this revenge all our lives."

"Oh thank you Ede! This means so much to me, you have no idea! Listen, this is the plan…"

The two women sat up all night discussing the details of the plan, and by daybreak, they sat smiling at each other, confident that finally, Willum would be avenged.

The day of the wedding came. The whole village was decorated with flowers and every villager within a five-mile radius had come to witness the priest's only daughter marry the Lord's son. Aelfric stood at the end of the aisle, waiting for his bride. Next to him was Edith's father, excited for his daughter's big day. The walls and floor of the church stood new and tall and proud, but the roof was yet to be finished, and the bright blue sky filled the church with light. The music started, and the bride, dressed in white and with her veil covering her face, began her slow walk up the aisle. The ceremony followed the traditional formalities of hymns and prayers, until the vicar intoned, "Do you Aelfric, take this woman Edith, to be your lawful wedded wife?"

"I do" replied Aelfic.

"Do you Edith, take this man Aelfric, to be your lawful wedded husband?"

"I do" came the quiet reply.

At that point, the veil was lifted, and panic followed.

Ede removed her veil, revealing that it had been her all along in that church. Aelfric was horrified, as were the priest and guests. Aelfric realised he has been tricked, and was now legally married to Ede, a homeless girl with no great looks. Before he could react, however, there was a cry from above. Standing on the eaves of the unfinished Church roof, stood Edith, dressed in all black, as if in mourning.

"Hear me, everyone" she cried, "This man is not a follower of God. You all know how terribly he treats the poor, his servants, all animals and anyone he deems to be below him. You know this and accept it because he is rich and his father is powerful and will protect him to all ends. You do not know, however, that he is a murderer!"

The gasps from below were loud even to Edith, and the mutterings she heard meant she knew she had their attention.

"This man, Aelfric, murdered Willum, as an act of vengeance when I first refused his hand. Willum was a kind and gentle soul, who did not follow our faith and yet acted more like a Christian than anyone in this Church. In jealousy, and because he knew he would not be reprimanded, Aelfric killed the love of my life. You now all know what he has done, but I do not believe he will stand trial. Instead let him live his life with the knowledge of what he has done, and what he has driven me to do. I swear on my life all this is true".

With these last words, Edith threw herself from the ledge, to the screams of the congregation, landing on the low altar right next to Aelfric, dead at his feet.

1348 AD

The Plague Comes to Titchfield

The Plague Comes to Titchfield

Margaret Thompson

Day One

It is the year of our lord 1348 and day one of our story (July 27th).

Rob hears that a boat is coming into Titchfield from France to unload the goods ordered by the Bishop of Winchester and the Abbot at the Abbey. It will then pick up grain, leather from the tanneries and wool from Titchfield to take back.

The Abbot has sent down timber and salt to send also.

Rob and his sister, Emma, feed the chickens and weed the vegetable patch. Rob takes his sister with him so his mother has the house clear to finish the washing for the merchant houses in the village.

He then dashes to the harbour. Sometimes he can earn money helping to unload. He overhears the Bishop's Stewards talking to the French sailors about a sickness that has appeared in Bordeaux, but they add that none of the sailors are ill.

Little do the villagers know that along with the brandy coming ashore, the French boat has brought tick-infested rats.

Rob is ten years old and lives with his mother Agnes and John Kech, his father, and also his big brother Simon aged 14 years, his sisters Emma, eight, and Joan, four, and his annoying baby brother Peter six months who seems to cry all the time.

His Father is a tenant farmer who pays his rent to the Abbot of Titchfield Abbey. He has four holdings and farms them with his three brothers. They live in cottages on their farms in the land alongside the River Meon, towards the Abbey. He has to do boon work alongside his fellow villagers two days a week on the demesne, the Abbot's land. On his own land he grows vegetables, grain for themselves and market, and grain for his hens and cows.

He and his brothers have sheep on the common, which is used by other villagers too. All their sheep have their own "Kech" brand. The wool is shipped to France by the village collective. All villagers pay a tithe to the Abbot for their exports. John also grows some herbs for Agnes who is the village expert on herbs and illness. She is the local midwife.

Rob makes his way home for his midday meal of pottage. He gives the farthing he has earned to his mother.

After his meal he helps her stretch the sheets. Once his sister has ironed them with the flat iron he and his sister will deliver them round the village to the merchant houses. The weather is good and his Dad comes home for lunch to ask him if he will come and help cut the barley.

Rob's other main task is to take the grain to the mill to be ground and watch over the milling to make sure he gets his full portion back after they pay their portion to the miller. He notes down the amount he gets to tell his mother.

Rob needs to keep busy as otherwise he can get up to mischief with the other boys in the village. His mother has to give him clear messages as he sometimes forgets what he has been asked to do.

The canon-vicar, Josef at Titchfield church, who is from the big Abbey up the road, comes to tea, this being the night when he teaches the local children to read and write. Rob is not that keen but his mother wants the children including the girls to learn as she had been taught when she was little.

Some of the other parents allow their children to come, boys and sometimes the girls too. The Kech cousins are there, and the Swein, Hirchon, and Friend children. They use tablets to write on and the bible to read. The cannon also has sheets he has prepared for the novice priests which he uses to teach the novices, when they first come to the Abbey.

The church is a meeting place for families when the daily toil is done. When the cannon is busy with the older children, teaching them to read and write, the little ones play on the floor and outside, dolls for the girls and toy boats and tops for the boys. The mothers gather and knit and watch the children, taking a well-earned rest.

Childhood is very short. They are absorbed into the workforce as soon as they are able, weeding, helping prepare vegetables, carding sheep fleeces.

Agnes though, does not often have time to rest: she was entrusted with a herbal written by a priest from Fontley village where she was brought up. This has lots of treasures inside, with details of herbs to use for the sick and in childbirth and with this trust comes responsibility

She is a secret source for women in pain or distress and when their children are ill throughout Titchfield and sometimes beyond. She can help them prevent conception, or aid them when another pregnancy would be too much. She also has charms for most things, encouraging a suitor, or helping a young girl to become pregnant.

Her knowledge is spread by word of mouth as she has to be careful not to attract the attention of the canons. She is saved from being branded as a witch as she is always helpful to families and refuses to be drawn into offering potions to do harm to warring neighbours.

She keeps a register of all the children born in the village, and how the birth was and if there had been any problem during the birth or after for the mother and child. This is helpful for her when the mothers fall pregnant again.

The weather is good for the next few days and the family manage to get all their barley, wheat and oats in and also the crops from the Abbot's land.

Titchfield is a thriving village, almost big enough to be a town. It has a weekly market. Tradesmen live in tenements in the street called West Street. They make ropes, card sheep fleeces ready to make rugs and spin wool. There are brewers and more than one house is a local place for men to drink. The tanners lived to the east of the village, as their job was smelly and messy, using urine and lime to cure the hides. They used the river to rinse their hides. Their work is really important as the hides are needed to make jackets and shoes, and also to sell them to France. The merchants live in bigger houses in the High Street and South Street. The tradesmen sell their goods at the weekly market in the Square and to merchants to ship the goods abroad.

Some trade in fish from the Abbot's fish ponds, with permission, and from the river. Others look after the salt pans, down by the sea.

A big harvest feast is held in the church on Lamas day, to celebrate the harvest with loaves of bread, fish and vegetables. The whole village comes, young and old, and dancing and drinking beer goes to until late.

This was going to be the last time that everyone in the Village was to be carefree and joyous for a long while to come.

Day Ten

There is an urgent knock on the door. William Swein, a friend of John comes to the door, distraught. "Come quickly my boy is ill, he is feverish, rambling and sick and he has a large lump under his arm".

Agnes gathers some herbs and runs out. Rob and Emma go to help. Sadly, despite cooling the child and giving him water and feverfew to try to bring down the fever, young Aidan dies. His mother catches the illness too, but, over the next few days, manages to survive though very weak.

As the days pass there are more calls for help as more children and adults become ill. Many have the symptoms. All have a fever, but some cough up blood and all those with the cough die.

Rob suddenly remembers the conversation he overhead from the sailors about illness in Bordeaux. He tells his mum, Agnes about this, and with her experience of illnesses she starts to worry that this is something new. Rumours begin to come through at the weekly market that the illness is appearing all over Hampshire, and lots of people are dying.

Agnes is selfless in her commitment to the people of Titchfield village. However she is starting to worry that she and her family might be in danger from her work with the ill families.

She has started herself to notice the pattern of symptoms and how these appear and progress over the illness period. All have a fever, but some cough up blood and all those that have those symptoms die quickly. She sits down to think things through and realizes that, in the last ten days ten people have become sick and of those six have died.

Both she and John are very scared. One night, after the children are in bed, John asks Agnes what she thinks is happening, He has noticed in the fields that the black rat population has increased and that many of them are dying too. Cats and dogs seem to be catching the illness as well, with their bodies adding to the rubbish in the streets. With Agnes telling him about the flea bites on the bodies of the sick and dying, they both finally agree that this might be an illness spreading through the rats. "We have to do more, John, otherwise I fear the whole village might die".

Day Twenty

John is a senior tenant farmer in the village and he calls a meeting, in the church. He asks the tenant farmers and representatives of the tradesmen and merchants. Many men are clutching sprays of lavender as a protection.

Not all come as they are scared to meet in company in case they get infected. Many of the merchants have already left to go and live in their lodgings in London.

Agnes and some of the older women from amongst the merchants and tradeswomen come also.

The whole village is banding together as the situation is beginning to look serious. John asks the men how many people do they know have died, and how many are ill? Rob writes it all down. John suggests that they try to keep a daily record as it looks like things are not going to go away anytime soon. Families are asked to report to John, or Rob if he is not there, whenever a family member becomes sick. . Many families have relatives in other villages and are beginning to worry about their health too; tradesman travelling with the Abbot's merchandise to Southampton, say that they have heard that the disease is all over Southampton and the villages in between. The word plague is beginning to be used to describe the illness that villagers have.

John tells them what Agnes has said, that this plague might be caused by fleas, as she has noticed bites on the bodies of the people who are infected or something from the rats, as there seem to be more of them about than normal. John says that she has been making us wash with Angelica when we come back from looking after the sick and she is suggesting that all do this. She says that she has read that Angelica might protect people from catching the plague. She has also been boiling all our undergarments when we take them off. She is also checking for fleas and putting crushed Pennyroyal or Rue in the clothes to discourage fleas. She has read in a pamphlet from a peddler that that is what the plague doctors are recommending. She has added Lady's bedstraw into the bedding to discourage the fleas. She is also working hard to keep the floors clean and has taken up the rushes from the floor.

She has been busy making potions and infusions and is teaching the girls how to do them. The boys when they are free from the farm work, are collecting any herbs she does not grow herself from the fields and woods. Their canon vicar has given her some Blessed Thistle from the Abbey, as the infusions are supposed to help cure the plague, according to the ancient books of the canons.

She says that the canon almoner, who is in charge of the Abbey hospital, has agreed to send advice and herbal information via the Titchfield canon to support her.

She asks the villagers if they can spare their girls and young boys; she will organize the gathering of the herbs and the making of infusions. Also she will teach them some skills to care for their sick families.

Agnes is exhausted and frustrated. "I have tried lots of different combination of herbs: lavender in the church to ward off evil; encouraging the villagers to grow feverfew round the houses to chew on to help the fevers; also to rub the floors of their house with rue juice to keep the fleas at bay. I have been administering to the sick infusions of pasque flower and butterbur to help the panic of people who are ill; poppy infusion to help relieve pain for those with boils; mallow flowers as a poultice".

"Some of the people falling ill do not have boils but have severe fevers, and are coughing up blood. I have tried feverfew to chew, to try to lower the fever and a little hollyhock potion for the coughing".

"Despite this, she says, people are dying and in the last two weeks four women, a man and four children died. There seems to be two types of the fever. Not all people who have the boils are dying, but they are very weak. It seems that those who have the symptoms of coughing and bloody sputum die very quickly in one or two days".

At the next Village meeting, led by Adam, a man who had lost his son and wife to this horrific illness, shouts out "there seem to be more rats than ever. I agree with Agnes. I wonder if the rats are the cause. They could have come in on the ships? Families are reporting getting bites and still we have not closed the port."

"Should we kill the rats?" they discussed how to do this without risking getting bitten or infected. Poisons made of hellebore can be put down. All families have cats to keep the population of rats down. But there seems to be too many rats and the cats and dogs are dying too.

Men were asked to volunteer to become rat catchers with heavy planks. They are going to wear cloths and leather wrapped round their legs. John said that she would ask Agnes to supply some black hellebore to poison the rats, but all were warned about keeping young children away from the bowls of hellebore.

Day Forty

Foreign Ships do not call any more. The Bishop is apparently not pleased, as his source of brandy has dried up. Agnes, however, the person who understands most about this illness, is secretly pleased. If this is where the rats are coming from, the boats being away might be the only way to get things under control again.

The number of dead has risen to forty.

John's sister and two of her children have died. Everyone has neighbours who have died and lost children. Agnes is delivering babies only to hear that they have caught the plague and died a couple of days later. The fear, panic and sadness is spreading as quickly as the illness that is causing them.

The men discuss whether they should close the weekly market, though they are worried how they will barter for goods. News is coming in from all over the county that whole villages are affected like Fareham, the next door village. One of the villagers had visited relatives in Quob, a village 13 miles away, and he said almost everyone seemed to be ill.

John asked how everyone was coping. Did anyone need support, were they managing their work-load and able to pay the rents. Were all children being looked after? Did any families need food?

The canon, Josef, who was friendly with Agnes and John has died himself, which was very sad as he was a good man. It also means that the community has lost its head vicar. Agnes herself is missing his wisdom and advice as she cannot help thinking that it is her that has let the villagers down. Could she have done more?

Day Sixty

James calls another meeting. The roll call of the dead has gone up to 70, with eight of the men dead and more women and children. Rob continues to write out the list to keep a record and so they know which families may need help to stop other members dying. People are taking in their relatives, although they are frightened, that by doing this, they might increase their own chances of catching it.

The children are very worried as some are too young to know what is happening. The older boys, some not very old at all, insist on coming to the meeting as they feel some responsibility too, especially those whose fathers have fallen to the plague.

Discussion becomes heated when someone suggests they should mark the houses where there is illness to stop people entering and catching it. Everyone felt as if they were abandoning the families inside to die.

As many men have died or are too ill to work, the farming tasks are divided up. The men are very angry as the bailiffs are demanding the rent and are not sympathetic to the families who cannot find the money.

The men discuss pooling their rents and to suggest to the bailiffs they could accept less from the village. If they all paid less, the bailiffs would not know what to do. They would have to accept this as they needed the tenant farmers to work the land.

Titchfield tenants have entered into arguments with the Abbot before about not being obliged to carry his grain to market, and won, so the villagers feel confident that this time they might persuade the bailiffs to be reasonable

Someone pointed out that the canons have now stopped giving last rights to those who are sick, as many of their number have fallen ill themselves and died. They also mentioned that all the canons at the church have left and retreated to the Abbey and so no services are running. Most families have even stopped gathering at the church socially, as they are scared to have contact with others in case they fall sick themselves.

Bravely, one of the young men who is planning to be a priest, spoke up and volunteered to hold services for those who wanted to come. He also said he would conduct burial services.

William asked "What should we do about the dead, who is going to bury them? And where?"

Everyone is scared: you could feel it in the room. Agnes, looking to John for permission to speak, told everyone again of her theory of how this illness was spreading. She had heard, from the canon almoner, that the best way of controlling this illness was to bury the dead quickly and isolate those who were sick from those who were well. "We must bury the dead and we must do it now"

Adam, whose whole family had died, said he would take responsibility "All my family have died I may have escaped it, I will bury the dead".

It was agreed that a pit would be dug some distance from the church as the dead had not had the last rites. The families are unhappy about this, but they pick a tranquil place with a view to the countryside not too far away. Some of the men volunteer to do the digging with Adam. Someone suggests putting lime in the pit, to try to keep the rats away. The belongings of the dead are also being routinely burned to try to stop the illness spreading. The dead rats and other animals in the streets were also put into the pits.

People are coming together again, thought John, we might get through this.

The culling of the rats was an ongoing task that took up everyone's time

Peter Hirchon, another senior farmer asks "Should we shut off access to the village? Should we stop people leaving?" Already families are leaving the village to stay with relatives up country, though messages coming back were full of terrible news of whole villages dying and even one, Quob, where no one was left. John tried to suggest this was a good idea, as Agnes had implored him to do this earlier; however there was mixed feelings due to the natural instinct to run away.

The older boys are to be put to the task of asking the mothers or sisters to make an inventory so there was enough food for everyone especially the families where no working men or boys are still alive. All the grain was in. The boys dug up roots and vegetables and buried them in a pit to try to preserve them

41

for as long as possible. The women gathered fruit, berries and nuts to try to curb hunger.

Everyone is distraught. John reads out a letter from the Bishop of Winchester, safe in his Wolvesey Castle, in Winchester, that says the illness is punishment from God because of the villagers' sins. The men become angry and shout, denouncing the priests saying that God has deserted them. They feel abandoned. Although this anger is high, it feels to John that relying upon God to save them might not be the best approach. If this final rejection from the Bishop can make the men save the village themselves then it might end up being a positive thing.

Agnes, her job done in explaining how they might control the spread of the illness to the men, went across to a local household where the women are meeting to discuss the plight of families, especially the children with dying or dead parents.

They talk about the food supplies and the women agree to pool their resources, despite what their men will say.

The women who understand and know the edible herbs and fruit, arrange for foraging parties, and the older women share recipes for pies and jams.

There are plentiful crops of apples, wild blackberries, strawberries and raspberries, in contrast to all the death in the village.

Edible herbs like thyme, sweetbay, sage, winter savoury and dandelions, are collected to make salads.

Fish were caught and salted to lay down for the winter.

At the moment there is still enough food to go round to make pottage and there is still flour for coarse bread.

Day Seventy

Village meeting: Fewer men gather for the meeting. Those that were still well enough were out looking after the sheep and shearing them for the women to card the fleeces to spin the wool. The meeting did not last long.

The chickens are still laying eggs but many have died. Agnes does not risk eating the dead chickens. Word is put out that no animals that died from disease should be eaten.

The only good news was that the Abbot's bailiffs are too scared to come to collect the rent. So the families are looking after each other, making sure that all have food, and are cared for

Despite all the nursing Agnes is well as are her older children. The things she had put into place at the start have worked. Sadly though, young Peter whom Agnes has tried to protect and find food for him, became ill. It was heart breaking for the whole family watching him die and to allow him to be taken to be buried in the communal pit. Even though Agnes herself, through John, was the person who started and continued to insist that this was done, she still wanted to break the rules. Life, and death, must go on.

Agnes and John have taken in his sister's two remaining younger children. They are very subdued but being with their cousins help. Their dad and the two older boys are struggling to keep the farm going. They come for their lunch with Agnes and the family.

Agnes is worried about her family in Funtley as many have died there. However little news is coming her way as finally, people have realized that traveling between villages is spreading the plague. Villagers have had to resort to violence at times to keep people out, and occasionally, to keep people in. Most of the residents of Titchfield, with John's lead, know that this is essential and take it in turns to patrol the perimeter of the village. But John is sure, despite their efforts, that people are still choosing to leave.

The Premonstratensian Abbey with the white robed canons at Titchfield has shut their doors and will give no more alms or succour to the poor. Another reason to keep strangers out. There is not enough to go around.

Day Eighty

The weather is growing colder, and the number of people becoming ill per week is going down. The men are cautiously optimistic. "All the work the women have been doing, keeping the houses clean, and washing the clothes has helped". There are less rats around.

Day One Hundred and Twenty

Discussions are held to decide how to try to get the goods to Southampton to sell. The Abbot wants to send his salt and timber. The villagers want to get some of the rugs and knitting the women have prepared to market. There is no spare food to send. Some of the villagers are concerned as they were trying to limit contact with outside villages.

As no foreign ships are coming, in the Abbot commissioned two boats and men are asked to volunteer to take the boats to Southampton.

Rob, Simon and a couple of the Sweyn and Cope men and their sons said they will go. They have sailed boats before and often Rob and Simon went too. Rob is going to take their mother's sheep rugs to sell.

The boat sets off weighed down by the cargo. The villagers wait anxiously for the boats return.

Five days later the boats returned with some good news and bad news. They have managed to sell the Abbot's salt and timber and the women's goods. Rob manages to get some material for the women to make clothes, and tools for the men folk.

The Abbot gets his brandy.

The bad news was that many in Southampton are very ill and there is no spare food to bring back.

It has been a hazardous journey with high seas, especially with the men being so weak and there is not a rush to repeat it.

Day One Hundred and Fifty

The weather grows colder; the days grow shorter; Christmas passes but there is not a lot of joy. All who want to, meet in the church and sing carols; the women do their best to make a festive meal. There is fish and potatoes and suet puddings.

As spring comes, the weather gets warmer and the illness comes back.

Men struggle to plant the summer wheat and grain.

Day One Hundred and Ninety

The meeting of the village men takes place as usual in the church. 60 of the village men have died and many of their wives and children. The rest are struggling to farm the land with the help of the older boys. The women, who are able, look after the orphaned children.

Some of the women who have nursed their family and survived, help out with nursing those that become sick.

There is despondency as the death rate starts to rise again.

Agnes's family is still intact but all are very frail. They and their neighbours are just struggling to survive. The rich merchants have died or left.

The miller struggles to mill the flour and some of the villagers go to help.

The men risk fishing from the Abbots ponds as the canons

remain in the Abbey and the Bishop's stewards do not visit anymore

The braver men poach rabbits as the villagers are hungry and desperate.

Life continues to be miserable and a continual struggle for survival.

Agnes brings together all the fit mothers and girls and they help each other to look after the children and cook and share the household tasks.

John has regular meetings with the men to try to support them and divide up the farming tasks and teach the young boys the skills they need to farm the land.

Instilling in them the hope that they will survive.

Agnes, when she has energy gets the children together to carry on teaching them to read and write, by encouraging them to write down the schedule for sowing the crops and the recipes for the women.

Day Two Hundred and Fifty
May 25th 1349

A Bailiff arrives from the Abbot to find a quiet, silent village. There are few tenements with smoke from the chimneys and many house are derelict.

He meets with John and the senior trade men to take a head count of the village. Only the tenant farmers and the tradesman who own their houses are counted.

130 tenant farmers have died and many tradesmen.

A large number of women and children have died also, according to John and Rob's figures there are at least 300.

The good news is that people are no longer dying. The recorded number of deaths from the plague has stopped.

The bailiff brings all the village together to discuss how they will get the fields working again and how to decide who should get the land of those who have died.

John and the men work out plans to get the village back on track.

As the women become stronger they clean out the houses, burning all the rushes from the floor and making up new mattresses with straw and Lady's bedstraw to discourage fleas.

Rob and Simon become stronger and help John who is tired and weak. Mary and Emma take on more tasks for Agnes and it looks like they will inherit their mother's skills with herbs.

John and his brothers and their sons take on more land.

Gradually the village returns to some kind of normality, and though sad about all those who have died, proud of themselves for surviving as a village group.

Ships return to the harbour. Will Rob go down to unload them again?

1494 AD

The Apostate

The Apostate

Peter Hiett

"Inquiry is to be made into the conduct of Brother Thomas Rubby, a quarrelsome fellow."

Brother Thomas was indeed on the quarrelsome side, but this was not what he wanted to hear.

The abbot, Thomas Coke, picked up the report on the visitation on Titchfield Abbey he'd received that morning, and waved it threateningly in Brother Thomas's direction.

"It says here we're generally well-run, apart from you. There've been Cokes in Titchfield for hundreds of years. I'm not having you ruin our good name. So improve your behaviour! Now get back to work in the fishponds."

"So much for for setting an example of humility," thought Brother Thomas as he made his way outside for the hours of cold and wet work that now lay ahead.

In truth, both men had some right on their side.

The abbot had just survived an inspection by the most frightening man he knew, Richard Redman - the man who ran the English branch of the Premonstratensian order of canons, from his base in distant Shap, in the far north-west. But he was more than head of his order. He was, most unusually, also a bishop. And even more unusually, he was the man the king sent for when he wanted difficult things to be done well. So when such a terrifying man found fault in in the way abbots were running his houses, abbots jumped.

But poor Brother Thomas felt badly treated. It was he who had with much difficulty persuaded the other canons to adopt his revolutionary ideas for ordering the abbey's library - one of the finest in England. It was he who had designed the channels which prevented the abbey's fishponds from silting up. And it was he who had gone to the trouble of learning French so his fellow-canons could better understand their rare collection of manuscripts from France. Was it his fault if others in the house were jealous of him? Why shouldn't he defend himself when criticised?

Even in comparatively rich abbeys such as Titchfield, life at the end of the fifteenth century was by no means simple. With little more than a dozen men in the house, conflicts broke out easily - there was no crowd in which to hide. The brothers had been more numerous, but repeated hammer-blows from the Black Death meant they had not regained their old numbers.

Still, the house had got off more lightly than some of its neighbours. For more than a century now the plague had been coming and coming again. It often took one person in five - children and young men first. One village near Titchfield lost all its inhabitants. The abbey's income was hit too - fewer people to pay it rent, fewer people to do its work. And the Premonstratensians -- or white canons, as they were sometimes called - were encouraged to go out into the world, to teach children and to treat the sick. This exposed them to further risk.

The results of the plague were profound. There were more orphans - some of whom sought homes in religious institutions, where they could be sure of at least getting fed. Thomas Rubby was one of these. But at the same time, the scarcity of peasants meant their labour became more prized. Feudal lords could no longer rely on feudal law to keep their serfs working, not when there were jobs to be had in towns and cities where their writ did not run. So if a monk - or a canon - decided to leave – there was really very little anyone could do about it.

In a lawless England still not fully recovered from the Wars of the Roses, almost anything was possible.

Such thoughts were bubbling at the back of the abbot's mind as he set about composing his response to the report of inspection.

My Lord Bishop

I thank you most humbly for the instructions you are kind enough to communicate to us. I shall of course endeavour to ensure that they are followed to the letter.

On the question of Brother Thomas - I wonder if I may crave your indulgence? He is indeed a most difficult brother. The other brothers complain about him frequently. As he does about them.

The issue is that he has far too lively a mind for this house to contain.

It has occurred to me that our Order might be better served if a better purpose could be found for him.

Might you, my Lord, in your many duties for our Order and our Lord the King, find a suitable way to put him to work?

He is ingenious, full of fancy, yet stubborn.

It is an ill mixture for our little House, so far from great deeds. Yet it may perhaps serve you?

Yours in Christ

Thomas Coke, Abbot

And so it was that three weeks later a letter arrived from Shap, and two weeks after that Brother Thomas found himself in the London palace of the Bishop of Winchester, a forbidding edifice set among the brothels and playhouses of Southwark. As Thomas knelt in the presence of the head of his order and of the Bishop of Winchester, the silence was broken only by the groans of prisoners in the bishop's own jail, the Clink.

"Boy, do you feel suited to a canon's life?" thundered Redman. He didn't wait for an answer. "I think I can employ you more profitably. Or do you prefer to spend the rest of your life building walls in Shap in the winter?"

For young Thomas, anything was better than wall-building and fishpond-tending. "My lord, I am at your service in whatever way you wish."

The two bishops glanced at each other.

"Good," said Redman.

And thus it was that for the next three years Thomas Rubby, no longer wearing the robes of a white canon, became a spy for the Order and for the king.

Posing as a Frenchman, he infiltrated and undermined the Cornish rebellions. Posing as an Irishman, he worked his way into Perkin Walbeck's confidence, even arranging for him to spend one week hiding in Titchfield. There was one riotous night which even now he blushed to think of, given the vows he'd taken. (But not as much as Betty Swain or Mary Hirchon should be blushing. Not that he thought they were capable of shame.) He even patrolled the Welsh Marches, still in intermittent rebellion despite having the Welshman Henry Tudor on the throne in Westminster.

But finally there came a day when he could hide no longer. The landlord of the inn where he was staying in Usk had started to ask him some rather pointed questions. And he'd learned enough Welsh to understand the whispers he heard in the inn's common room. So he left, as if to relieve himself - then ran for his life, up the hill, into the castle. It was the longest run of his life, and nearly his last. As he pounded at the postern an arrow bounced off the granite at his shoulder. But the gate opened, and he was in and safe.

The castellan of Usk gave him an armed escort for the long ride to Southwark. There, he once again resumed the white habit of a premonstratensian canon. And in due course, with the blessings of the bishop of Winchester, he made the slow, and now much safer, return to Titchfield Abbey.

And though Abbot Coke gave him a warm if somewhat nonplussed welcome, the fishponds and even the library had lost what little lustre they ever had. He studiously avoided Betty Swain and Mary Hirchon.

So passed a year, quietly, and to tell the truth, rather boringly.

Until Richard Redman came to make another visitation. It was 1497.

"You did very well for me my boy. Are you happy now? Settled?"

"Well my Lord, I am as ever at your service. And yet, I wonder if you might have another use for me?"

The bishop thought for a moment.

"I believe I do. It's dangerous -- unpredictable - but your life will never be the same again. Tell me boy, what do you know about ships?"

"My lord, my father was a fisherman until the Black Death took him. I often ventured with him beyond Wight as far as France or Devon searching for the shoals. I am as handy on a boat as a sparrow in a tree."

"Good. Well you won't have heard of this, but John Cabot is shortly to set sail to discover and claim new lands in the Indies for the King. He leaves from Bristol in two months. I don't trust him in the slightest. I want you on his ship, and if any of you survive, I want a full report. I need to know what's happened.

"You'll have to do your best to make sure he loses no time though. I hear some mountebank called Amerigo Vespucci is planning to do the same for Spain.

"Cabot may be unreliable, but he's all we've got."

Brother Thomas blinked as a shaft of sunlight came through the library window.

"Yes my Lord. And my position here?"

"We can't have people knowing about this. I'll mark you down as run away. There's altogether too much of this kind of thing. No-one will give it a second thought."

So the bishop's report on his visit formally marked down Thomas Rubby as an apostate – and Thomas himself set out for Bristol with a letter of introduction from the Bishop to John Cabot. Cabot knew what was good for him – and decided to make use of his unexpected crewman's educated intellect to help him with his navigation. With a crew of only 18, Cabot needed as much brainpower at his side as possible. And the intelligent and imaginative Rubby could certainly supply that.

Like Columbus and Vespucci, Cabot was looking for a safer route to the riches of the Indies, one that would bypass the growing dangers from the Ottoman empire, which only a few decades earlier had captured the great city of Constantinople, and now controlled all the main trade routes from Asia to Europe.

The future of spice and silk was at stake, he believed.

They set off from Bristol, sailed west across the Atlantic – a terrifying experience for Thomas, who knew only the comparative calm of the English Channel – and then north. The tiny craft, the Matthew, seemed ill-suited to the huge task ahead.

In the few spare moments his duties allowed him Thomas kept a journal – written in code, of course – and made sketches for the bishop of the wondrous things he saw: whales, dolphins, and once an albatross, weeks away from land, hanging silent and still above them. He watched as his crew mates' teeth fell out and the men fell sick – sailors knew what scurvy was, but not how it was caused or how to cure it.

Eventually they sighted land – a bleak, unwelcoming tract. For the crew, it represented a chance for survival. They anchored in a bay and went ashore by longboat. Cabot proclaimed the land Newfoundland in the name of the King. No-one heard the ringing proclamation except the crew, who cheered dutifully.

Thomas wasn't at all sure that they'd discovered a new part of the Indies. The unforgiving landscape in front of him bore little resemblance to the lush lands he'd seen described in the writings at Titchfield Abbey.

Cabot took the chance to re-victual his vessel. Fresh water to replace the rank liquid currently festering in his casks. Meat from the bears and caribou found along the shores, butchered and preserved in brine on the beach. Cod from the shoals teeming in the sea -- And whatever fruits and vegetables and berries that could be found and stored.

Cabot spent some time drawing charts – the most valuable item any mariner possessed. Thomas did the same. Then, with the scurvy abated, they set sail for home.

Back in Bristol, Rubby pocketed his pay and set off for Winchester Palace in Southwark. Now he was a guest rather than a canon, so was spared the duties of a religious life and was able to enjoy the entertainments which surrounded the Palace – and from which the Bishop profited.

After a month of dissipation as guest of the bishop, Rubby was down to his last few pennies when the head of his order came to call.

"Good work, Thomas," Richard Redman said after reading the report and studying Thomas's charts. "Heaven knows why we keep describing these lands as the Indies. It's plain to me they're nowhere near.

"Still, that's no longer your concern. Tell me, now that you're an apostate, how will you fill your days?"

"I had hoped, my Lord, to return to Titchfield – though not as a canon."

"And perhaps not as Thomas Rubby either, I'll warrant."

"Indeed not, my Lord."

"I think the Order can supply you with the wherewithal to live there as gentleman. And with a new name too."

"Thank you, my Lord."

"I hope I shall be able to call on you in the future, Thomas. God gave you talents which it would be a sin to waste."

"Of course, my Lord. Thank you"

The man who used to be Thomas Rubby lived long and happily in Titchfield. He ran his estate well and treated people decently. His stewards did the same during his occasional absences. On his return, he'd simply say he'd been away on his Lord's business. No-one quite knew who this Lord was. But no-one was quite brave enough to ask – it was plain that he did not wish to share his secrets, and this was a man who kept his weapons sharp – not that anyone in Titchfield ever saw him use them.

Thomas lived long and happily in Titchfield. And even if villagers sometimes wondered at this man who would walk along the Meon to gaze at the sea, apparently with longing in his eyes, none guessed that he was thinking of a long-ago voyage to a far-away land, where bear and caribou roamed the shores, and the sea boiled with fish never seen in Titchfield.

1537 AD

Letters from a Novice

Letters from a Novice

Margaret Pace

In the year of our Lord, 1537
The tenth day of December

My dearest Mother,

You will be surprised to receive this letter as you know that I am not usually allowed to write to you more than twice a year. However, we are living in dramatic times and the Abbot has given all the novices special dispensation to write to tell our parents what is happening to us and the Abbey at Titchfield.

We are all praying that the King will reconsider the drastic step that he is proposing of defying Rome in divorcing the Queen. We fear it will lead to a break with Rome and our Catholic faith. If the worst happens, then our beloved Abbey will be taken over by the crown and, probably, given to a nobleman for services rendered to his Majesty's cause.

What will happen to the Roman Catholic priests we have no knowledge, but rumour has it that we shall all be sent abroad. I cannot imagine leaving this lovely place. It is only now, when we are on the verge of losing our way of life, that I am really appreciating all that we have in this little corner of England.

The garden has been extraordinarily productive this

year and we have been enjoying an abundance of God's gifts. The peaches, growing on the south wall, have produced the best crop for years and Father Anthony has put down many firkins of his special brew. I hope we may be allowed to take it with us, but I think it unlikely.

The fish ponds have been a source of delight for me, you know how I love fishing, and the hours I have spent at the upper pond, providing food for our table, has given me the luxury of communing with God in His own garden. The wild flowers in the meadows have been especially beautiful and the honey combs in Father Leo's bee boles have overfilled with their golden treasure. This we have carefully preserved in jars, and it will keep for many months.

The harvest, because of the early rain, was good this year and the fields have yielded well. The barn behind the Abbey is full of corn and hay, enough to last the winter and beyond. All this bounty, I fear, we shall soon have to leave.

Father Francis has been spending many hours in the library binding up our precious books. Our library is the finest in Southern England, so we believe. We pray continually for God's guidance and trust in Him to keep us safe. The schoolroom is empty, the villagers are reluctant to send their children to us for fear of retribution. Father Leo is lost without the little ones around him, and continually asks "Who will teach the children, now, the word of God?"

Father Thomas, the canon vicar, returned yesterday in great distress, his beloved church of St. Peter's has been vandalized and the statues and hangings all destroyed. Can this destruction really be so that the king can marry again? That, surely, cannot be the whole story. We hear rumours that the Abbey is too profitable and the lands too valuable for our own good. We have heard that the King is greatly in need of funds for his army, perhaps that is his reason.

Father Thomas has retired to his bed and is inconsolable. We are praying for his sanity.

Our newly appointed Abbot, John Salisbury, has been called to Winchester by the King's Commissioners and will journey there on the morrow. We are anxiously awaiting news. We are sad to think what might become of us as we prepare to go our separate ways. It is unlikely that we shall all be together.

I must stop now as it time for Vespers, God willing, I will continue this on the morrow...

My dear Mother, it is over a week since I last was able to write and there has been little time, and opportunity, to continue this letter to you. The Abbey has been in a state of turmoil.

We had news from London, dreadful news, that over one hundred nuns at the convent at Tyburn have been put to death. We find it hard to comprehend such brutality. How the poor nuns must have suffered before they came into the Lord's presence. May they now rest in peace.

The Cannns are uneasy for us novices, who work outside the Abbey walls, but we have had no animosity shown us by the local villagers.

They seem to fear only the soldiers, with some reason. How will it all end? We are in God's hands. If we are to be split up and sent abroad we may never see each other again. It is hard for us all.

I have more sad news to impart, Father Thomas has

died. I think of a broken heart. He could not bear to see his beloved Church desecrated, it was all too much for him.

His funeral will be tomorrow and, as the Parish Vicar, he will be buried in the Churchyard. We will process from the Abbey.

Our Abbot returned from Winchester with the news that he will have to surrender the Monastery to the King's Commission on December 28th. We have been ordered to send our thousand precious books to Winchester, together with the plate and any other precious chalices we use for communion. We are all devastated. I have no heart to continue this eve, we are in shock.

Pray for us dearest Mother. I will write when I know where I will be.

Your loving son, in Christ,

Michael.

The tenth day of January in the year of our Lord 1538

Dearest Mother,

I write to let you know that I am safe. I know that you will have been concerned for my welfare over the last weeks and forgive me for the worry I must have caused you, but this the first opportunity I have had to write. The White Canons had been in our beloved Monastery for over 300 years, so there was much to be done as we all prepared to leave on 28th December. It has been an emotional and exhausting time.

I have been very fortunate in obtaining a position with the new Vicar at St. Peter's Church! God has indeed looked with favour on his unworthy servant. I will be assisting the Vicar settle into his new position in Titchfield, but my main occupation will be caring for the churchyard. The River Meon lies to the East of the Church and I have been granted permission to fish there, which fills me with delight. In the meantime, I am temporarily lodging with a farrier who used to help us bring the harvest in.

The Canons and the other two novices have been sent to other Monasteries in France. They travelled in a small boat from Titchfield two weeks ago. Our farewells were painful, but I am consoled by the knowledge that they will all be safe over the channel.

Now, I have a secret to impart to you, a very important secret, that must be kept to yourself, you must tell no one, if you do your life could be in danger so please. Mother, heed me. When we carried Father Thomas to St. Peter's Church for burial, we secreted a silver plate and a Chalice, in a small sack, in his coffin. Once the service had been completed and all the villagers had left and before we filled in the grave, we removed the sack and put it at the foot of the coffin. I am now the only person in England who knows that it is there, except for you now, dear Mother. I am not sure if there will ever come a time when it will be right to dig up these precious religious pieces, but, in the future, with another king on the throne, Catholicism might return to England, and we will be able to return the silver to its rightful place on a Catholic altar. Keep this in your heart, dear Mother. If I should die before you then you must confide this secret to someone you can trust.

As I no longer belong to a holy order, I hope that I shall have the new Vicar's permission to visit you sometime during the year, that would be such a joy to me, to see you and my dear brothers and sisters again.

God Bless and keep you, my dearest Mother, you are always in my thoughts and prayers.

Your loving son, in Christ,

Michael

1537 AD

The Altar Cloth

The Altar Cloth

Rosa Johnson

It was a wretched life, being a pot boy. He was at the beck and call of everyone in the New Inn. They weren't very kind to him. They called him Orphan Tom and he hated it. He and his sisters worked for scraps and barely kept themselves alive.

His only solace was the church, where he could find peace. But even the church was in turmoil. The Church of England had broken from Rome, and a lot of people enjoyed the licence this allowed.

He heard the clatter of hoofs, and then a platoon of soldiers burst into the Inn. They had ridden hard, and needed to quench their thirsts. They were tired, and as they relaxed under the influence of the ale they became crotchety, looking for trouble. They began by criticising the church in general and St. Peter's in particular. St. Peter's was a long established and rich church, with beautiful stained glass windows, statues in niches and lovely wall hangings.

They hoped for a reaction from the village men and were surprised by the one they got. The villagers were not at all pleased with the church. The church laid onerous obligations on them, and they saw a chance to get rid of it altogether. They encouraged the soldiers in their complaints.

"I say we have no more graven images." There was a brief pause while the men around the table considered this. Jethro raised his voice, "I say again, we shall have no more graven images!"

Barnaby sucked at his clay pipe. He spoke sagely. "You speak the truth there, Jethro, 'tis in the Commandments"

The villagers applauded. "I'll drink to that. Have another jug of ale"

The laughter rose as the drinks flowed. The soldiers were not bad men, but were egged on by the villagers. They saw the chance of a bit of fun and perhaps some looting. After all, Catholics were lawful game.

"Hey you" said Jethro, "show us which of the houses here belong to Catholics. We'll have a go at them first, and then we'll start on the church."

Thomas Swain thought it prudent to leave the New Inn and go to the church. Perhaps he could warn the vicar. Crouched low, behind the altar, trembling with fear, Thomas cradled his head in his hands and prayed like he had never done before.

'Dear God, deliver me from the evil of the King's Army,' he whispered, 'Holy Mother, keep me safe that I may live to care for my sisters; and please keep them out of danger,' he added.

The great wooden door at the back of the church was flung wide with a resounding crash which echoed throughout the building. The clatter of horses' hooves on the flag stones in the church porch was heard. Terrified worshippers fled screaming, trying to escape the horsemen storming into the building and going about the business of destroying St Peter's Holy Church, and the people in it.

The sounds of unremitting destruction rent the boy's ears as sacred ornaments were swept from their pedestals, glass in treasured windows was shattered, sacred paintings were despoiled, wall-hangings slashed and ripped to shreds as men wielded swords and axes, smashing decorative niches and rich ornamentation in God's house. Thomas put his hands over his ears and kept his head down as men shouted and laughed, swelling the clamour.

The boy had entered from the graveyard, unseen. He had heard the King's Horsemen advancing down East Street when he was putting ox-eye daisies on his mother's grave. He had picked them from the roadside for her because he remembered how she loved them.

The Infantry was marching through the village setting fire to houses of Catholics as they came. The boy had to find cover. He had to save his own life so that he could return to their home afterwards and look for his two little sisters. Surely soldiers of any faith would spare two innocent little girls.

Moving swiftly and silently between the graves he made for the priest's door knowing it would be open and he would be safe inside. Quickly he slipped into the shadows among the statues of saints in the chancel and concealed himself behind the altar. Had his life not been in danger he wouldn't have dared go so near to the statue of the Holy Virgin but now he would look to her for protection.

The church, usually a place of peace and meditation, today was filled with a deafening noise as it was ransacked by a band of villainous intruders. The air was thick with dust and Thomas feared he might cough or sneeze, 'Holy Mary, please keep my mouth silent,' he prayed.

He had sought refuge in the church before but there was little solace here today,

Royalists were smashing it to pieces and they had no right. He wished he was more than ten years old and big and strong enough to confront them. He was frightened but for his sisters' sakes he must be brave.

What was happening now? The sacred screen crashed to the floor and men were laughing; yes, they were elated by the destruction and devastation they were wreaking.. Thomas crept further under the altar cloth and years of accumulated dust and damp reached his nostrils. He stifled a sneeze pinching his nose so hard it brought tears to his eyes. The terrible cacophony around him made him fear for his life. If he was found he'd never see his sisters again.

Thomas couldn't believe what he was hearing. Someone was on the steps in front of the altar shouting oaths as he wielded an axe. Shall I be found and killed? Is this my last hour? he wondered. The assailant swung the axe again, grunting with the effort; the altar yielded and went over backwards. The wood cracked and splintered in pieces around the boy. He crouched even lower lest his head shaped the damaged fabric and he was discovered.

Gradually the noise lessened, voices were retreating, someone called to the few soldiers remaining in the church to leave. They had done a good job. The one nearest the desecrated altar gave it a final kick and joined his triumphant friends. Thomas trembled in a stifling peace beneath the heavy altar cloth while the dust settled around him. He was too terrified to move now but he was still alive and thankful for his deliverance.

The boy wanted to take a deep breath but the air was full of dust and the smell of smoke seeping in from the burning buildings in the street was acrid and painful to his nostrils and his lungs. He lifted the altar cloth above his head and crept out from the safety of his hiding place.

He saw the devastation in the church and rays of the sun picked out thick clouds of dust motes rising into the lofty roof of the nave. He coughed as it reached his throat. Picking his way carefully through heads, hands and feet of broken statues, he made his way back to the priest's door but it was off its hinges and wouldn't open.

Thomas went slowly towards the main door of the church. He could see a woman standing there and was afraid because he felt sure she was weeping.

'Dear God, what can I do for this woman?' he prayed. As he went forward she reached out her hand gently touching his head. She wiped his tear-stained face with the end of her blue sleeve.

Thomas was overwhelmed. He looked up into the face of a beautiful lady and saw it was The Virgin Mary, herself. He fell to his knees bowing his head, and putting his hands together.

'Holy Mother,' he murmured.

Taking his arm in her cool fingers she raised him to his feet again. She led him towards the door. In a voice like an angel's she said, 'Go safely, my child.' Her sweet face lifted Thomas's spirit and he felt stronger.

The boy was afraid of what he had seen and heard. He wanted to glance behind but daren't until he was through the door.

When he eventually looked back the angel in blue had gone. Only a damaged statue remained. It toppled and fell, shattering into a thousand pieces.

1572 AD

Wet Nurse for the Heir

Wet Nurse for the Heir

Rosa Johnson

'Is our guest in good health today, Mary?' Henry asked.

'I have not seen her today, Henry. She will see nobody save her physician and her nurse,' said his wife. 'On no account may anyone enter her bed-chamber. Henry she is so distressed I fear for her sanity!'

'She'll soon recover, Mary. Women are made to bear the pain of childbirth.' Henry's glib response belied his concern for the Lady Elizabeth, who was in her forty first year, and for the child who if male would be his heir.

When Henry, the 2nd Earl of Southampton told his wife, their Queen wished to reside with them in Ticefeld for two or three months, Mary agreed willingly, she felt she owed something to her friend. At the dissolution of the monasteries her father, King Henry VIII, had given the three hundred year old Abbey and estates they now held to The Earl's father in recognition of his faithful service. The Abbey became Place House, the Southampton family seat.

Henry and Elizabeth had grown up together in the Royal Household. In adulthood Henry remained close to advise her on personal and national affairs. The Queen attended his marriage to Mary Browne and frequently stayed at their homes on the south coast and in London. Elizabeth was their monarch and friend.

In the winter sunshine Henry left the house to join his cohorts hunting wild boar in the oak forests. His wife watched him go astride his favourite mount. He called to the hounds and shouted orders at the top of his voice to other riders. He had already forgotten his guest.

With her fingers in her ears Mary ascended the stairs to the first landing. Unhappy sounds and cries of pain from the bedchamber were abating now and she heard... yes, the first cry of an infant recently emerged from a mother's womb. Almost at once the physician opened the bedroom door swept onto the landing and hurried down the broad stone staircase..

'Sir, is The Lady Elizabeth...?' He did not stop but as he left the house he called out, 'She has a son, Madam. In my opinion, not the first bastard to emerge from those 'virgin' loins! '

The child could be heard as Mary respectfully knocked the heavy oak door. The mid-wife's voice commanded her to wait. She pictured the scene; the fire burning on the hearth, bowls of hot water, steam, bloodstained linen and the baby. He cried lustily. Was Elizabeth in the same rude health as her child Mary wondered. It was perhaps unlikely since age was against her.

'Enter!' Elizabeth's frail voice interrupted Mary's musings. She almost ran to the door. Peering round it, she saw her dear friend relaxing against deep pillows, pale but apparently in fair spirits.

'Madam,' she dropped a curtsey.

'Mary, did you a hear him? What a voice! The noisy brat. Just like his father, ...' .Her Majesty's lip curled slightly into a smile. 'But Mary, that is a part of the story to which you are not privy.'

'Mary Browne we must have a suitable wet nurse for the boy.' I would have you engage one from among your friends.' Mary was taken aback. 'Madam it will no doubt be possible to find a wet nurse in our village.' She wondered why the Queen had expected wet nurses to be among her friends and why she had taken to addressing her aggressively as Mary Browne. Did she think any of her friends would deign to act as wet nurse for this child presently clamped to his mother's breast, or for that matter to any other babe? The mid-wife was busy clearing away the debris of the birth when Mary asked if she knew of a wet nurse who would oblige the Lady Elizabeth.

'I will find one Madam, with milk enough for five. She will come tomorrow.'

'When will Henry return?' the Queen demanded.

'Henry will not return until sundown, My Lady. He will feast with his cohorts in the village.' She paused. 'May I suggest some warm broth be brought from the kitchens for you Madam?'

Elizabeth dragged the child from her breast and handed the tightly wrapped bundle to Mary.

'And now you may acquaint yourself with your new son and heir Mary Brown.' Mary took the child and gently mopped the whimpering, puking mouth. 'Remember, tomorrow he will be yours and I will prepare to return to London as soon as I am able. — My maid will fetch me a little broth.'

Mary knew the Queen's most ardent wish was to return to Hampton Court and put the memory of the birth of the child behind her. She had successfully concealed her pregnancy from her household except for those closest to her and by spending the last three months in Hampshire with only her personal maid, few had suspected. In Henry's House she had insisted on being known as The Lady Elizabeth and reference was never made to her supreme authority.

The Queen had no desire to acknowledge the child in her court but she could not make better arrangements for him than as the Southampton heir. As the country's unmarried virgin queen presentation of a son and heir to her subjects would be, to say the least, unpopular.

Mary smiled at the child in her arms. He was a fine boy, as like her own daughters as peas in a pod. He stirred in his sleep and she warmed to him knowing she would grow to cherish him. If Henry insisted he should become a part of the Royal household she would spend time in their Holborn house so she and her daughters could be near their little brother. It would be good for them to see something of London life and of the Royal Household too.

'When Henry returns we shall introduce him to his son and heir.' Mary said. 'He has long urged me to produce a son for him. Your confinement has alleviated his pressure on my body for which I am truly grateful.

'Had God not invented the excitement of the bedchamber, Mary, few women would choose to give birth. I insist we remain in close touch.' She paused showing signs of fatigue. 'He shall be christened Henry. The Queen closed her eyes and lay back on her pillows. Now I must rest. You may go Mary Browne.'

Mary curtsied to her Queen the way she had been taught and as she turned to go she said, 'Your secret is safe in my heart, Your Majesty, I will say nothing.'

1602 AD

The Titchfield Witch

The Titchfield Witch

Hannah Hiett

It was a bright, breezy morning in early spring and sunlight streamed through the oak and hawthorn leaves, dappling the dirt road. Pools of sunlight flashed over the grey stone and wood cottages as the wind stirred the old boughs over the lane and Old Ma Howell made her way home.

She had spent the morning in the copses and hedgerows around the village gathering wild herbs, liquorice root, loveage and lavender to refill her store and prepare a special remedy. Kit Swain the tanners' boy had visited her cottage the previous morning, pale-faced, fidgeting with the rim of his broad-brimmed hat, and nursing an ache in his heart.

"Good morning Ma Howell, how do you do?"

"I am very well Kit, though I fear the same can't be said for you if that moon-calf face is much to go by."

She laughed kindly, standing in the low doorway of her stone cottage and framed by a creeping rose that wound its way above the lintel.

"I fear I am ill mistress, gravely so. I don't sleep, I can't take any bread. I am bewitched."

"Is that so now? And whom, may I ask, is the wicked sorceress who is responsible for this bewitchment?" Ma Howell's blue eyes were twinkling with amusement but poor Kit looked horrified. "Oh no Ma, please I only meant it as a fancy of speech. I would never accuse anyone of anything so... so foul and wicked as..." he drew breath and whispered, "witchcraft... and especially not..."

Ma Howell chuckled. "I know what you meant lad, don't you fret. I think you'd better come inside."

Old Magret Howell had lived in Titchfield village since the day she was born, in the same stone cottage at the end of the lane where she had always been. And all the villagers knew to find her there should they be in need. Magret had been born the same year as Queen Elizabeth herself, which was how she knew that both Queen and subject were approaching their 70th year, an age impressive for princes, and quite extraordinary for ordinary country folk. Some said it was her good heart that kept her so strong and well, others hinted - always with affection – that the devil had something to do with it most likely.

Magret Dymmok, as she was then, had been married at 15 and had given birth to nine children, three of whom had survived infancy. Tomas, her eldest, had gone to sea and died of a sweating fever in the New World. Alice had married, travelling with her husband to find work in London, and had died in childbed in a stranger's care. Robert, her youngest, had stayed in Titchfield to be apprenticed as a blacksmith, until the day he was kicked by a visiting nobleman's horse and killed outright.

In the forty years since her husband's death, Magret Howell made her living as a midwife and healer – making use of the great knowledge of herbal remedies taught to her by her own mother and grandmother. She had helped bring almost every soul in the village into the world, which is how she had come to be known by the world that she knew as Ma Howell.

Not long after poor Kit had left the warmth of her kitchen

to return to the tannery at the north end of the village, Ma Howell had set about her preparations only to be interrupted by a second knock on her door.

A young woman stood there, gold curls peeking out from under her cap and a furious blush spreading across her face, red as a holly berry.

"Good day Ma Howell, I hope I am not bothering you?"

"And why would a visit from you bother me Mary Stokes? It's always a pleasure to see you on my doorstep." Magret smiled a broad welcoming smile, but inside she was laughing. "Is everyone well at home?"

"Oh yes madam, very well I thank you. You see, that is, well, was that Kit Swain I saw leaving your house just now? It's only that – uh – my father wanted to speak to him about some leatherwork, I suppose, and so sent me to fetch him you see, and so I wanted to know if he was... busy." At this red-faced lie, Magret burst out laughing, great guffawing peals of delight that sent the thrushes in the hedgerows fluttering into the sky.

"Come in my girl, I have just the thing you need I'm sure."

Come mid-summer Kit Swain and Mary Stokes were wed at St Peter's by the old curate. At the wedding breakfast, a curious story was told of how the bride and groom had each planned to poison the other with a love philtre – mysteriously acquired – only to find by the end of that spring that both were already quite in love with the other anyway. Bride and groom laughed along with the tale and Ma Howell sat at one end of a long bench, in a cool corner of the inn, laughing along with them. Only she knew that her 'philtre' had been nothing more than rain water, rosemary from her neat kitchen garden, a little wild lovage root and a dab of honey for sweetness.

The dancing and merriment continued into dusk and as the light faded the happy couple were seen off with whoops and cheers and catcalls and giggles into Kit's father's tannery on South Street to begin their married life proper. The unmarried girls placed wreathes of flowers on the heads of the newlyweds and, once they were gone, the farm-hands, apprentices and village dandies rushed up to ask the prettiest of them to dance.

In the midst of this scene, a stranger appeared in the doorway of the inn. He was very tall and very thin and wearing the plain black traveling clothes of a clergyman. He had a face that might have been handsome, but the pallidity of his skin and the deep circles under his eyes spoke of sleepless nights spent poring over books, papers and pamphlets. He surveyed the room, decked out as it was with crushed and faded flowers, spilled ale and the bare-armed, bare-headed dancers whirling and laughing. "I see there is much work for me to do. May the Lord give me the strength to accomplish it to his satisfaction." He muttered low to himself.

"Inn keeper?" he called, "I will be needing a room for the night, it happens the Vicarage is not yet ready for me – it is my fault, I am earlier than promised and essential repairs are still being made."

"Of course, Your Grace, I will arrange a room for your right away. And may I say, welcome to Titchfield. Ellen! Make up our best room for his Eminence, quickly now!"

"No need for the honorifics man, I'm neither a bishop nor a papist." The stranger spat this last word with a vehemence that took the inn-keeper by surprise.

"Apologies my... um..." The inn-keeper's eyes darted about in desperation. He looked pleadingly at the assembled wedding guests, who were now quite quiet and still, staring at the bat-like apparition of the new Vicar of Titchfield, who filled the doorway like a figure of Death himself.

"I am the Reverend Francis Bradsell, you may address me as Reverend Bradsell. I am to take over the post of Vicar from my late respected colleague the Reverend William Parker, may God preserve his soul."

Francis Bradsell glared in disapproval around the tavern once more and followed the inn-keeper up the stairs two at a time.

In a small chamber overlooking the village square, Bradsell lit a tallow candle and sat with his elbows on a small table, fingers steepled as though in prayer. It had been an uneventful four days ride south from Cambridge. He had slept in clean, well-kept inns, travelled only in daylight and kept to the King's roads, wary of brigands and thieves. Nothing at all remarkable had occurred until he was just a mile or two outside the village, weary from a long day on horseback. The light was fading at last and the sky was a midsummer turquoise like the Indian Ocean. As his horse approached Titchfield from the Fareham road, he passed a woman walking in the same direction. She could not yet be twenty years old and she walked with a light, tripping step that belied the miles of dust and dirt on her shoes and the hem of her dress. A few dark red tresses had escaped her cap and tumbled over her pale neck. When she turned, Francis Bradsell's heart stopped beating, just for a moment, then resumed it's pulse faster than if he had run the length of the lane to catch her. Her eyes mirrored the green-blue of the sky, like church glass in the old cathedrals and the every-day churches of France and Italy, churches he had never seen. He imagined that he could almost smell the sea from here.

The young woman smiled and curtsied to him, there on the side of the road. Bradsell, disturbed, tore his gaze away from her face with an effort, dug in his spurs and galloped towards the first evening lights of the village.

Now, Francis Bradsell meditated on that face, that fall of hair, the brightness of that skin. He thought idly of his colleagues and mentors at Cambridge, and their plan to petition to the Queen to allow the English clergy to marry once more, just as soon as her Majesty was past this latest illness... then kicked himself. If the petition were ever to be put forward, and accepted, and law changed – he, Francis Bradsell, would marry, certainly. But he certainly could not marry the sort of girl who might be found all alone after nightfall by the side of the road. No, if she were a parishioner of his, she would be no different from the others, and if she were simply passing through, all the better.

With that decision firm in his mind, Bradsell prepared for bed and the new day, congratulating himself on overcoming the first hurdle the devil had placed on his righteous new path.

Ma Howell was rarely surprised, she had lived too long and seen too much in her life to be often caught unawares. The wedding party had surely taken a strange turn with arrival of the new Vicar, but nothing could have prepared her for what she found sitting on her doorstep as she came up the lane in the moonlight. "God in heaven, Alice, is that you?"

It was a ghost. A ghost with milk-white skin, dark red hair and Alice's blue-green eyes, waiting outside the cottage for Magret's return.

The ghost looked just as surprised as Magret and leapt to her feet. "No madam! I am Kathren Kemp. Alice Kemp, or Alice Howell if you like, was my mother. If you are Magret Howell then I am your grand-daughter. I have been been waiting for you here since nightfall, a carter on the bridge told me this was your house."

"Heavens, I believed the spirit of my own Alice was walking the earth and had come for a visit. But, can you be Alice's daughter? I did not know my poor girl had a child living! I heard of her death but I believed that her child had not survived, least no-one told me any different." Magret paused, amazed, and felt anger rising in her. "Curse your pox-ridden weasel of a father for never bringing you to me or sending news of you! How could he!"

"It is no use to curse him now madam," replied Kathren sadly, "for my father is dead already. He told me during his last days that I must come to you as my only family living. He said that though you may have hated him, you wouldn't turn me away, for my mother's sake you wouldn't. I have walked a long distance and I'm very tired, I hope I am welcome."

Ma Howell stared at her grand-daughter a moment, then strode forward, grabbed Kathern Kemp by her shoulders and pulled her into a firm hug.

"Welcome?! Heavens of course you are welcome child! Now, first thing's first, let's find you something to eat, you look half dead from famishing!"

Summer rolled into Autumn, the harvest came and went and whispers of the Queen's failing health began to reach the ports, the taverns, the markets, the fields, cow-sheds and cottages too, until her Majesty was in every child's nightly prayers.

In the village, life went on as it always had, full of small joys and trials. Kit and Mary Swain were expecting their first child in the coming spring, Old Nathaniel Swain had begun to feel the cold in his bones more and more, a cow grew sick and died on the Democks' farm and Tomas Thwaites' lad fell from a tree and broke his leg. There were weddings too, once the Harvest was over, but these were very sober affairs under the stern eye of Reverend Bradsell.

In Ma Howell's cottage, preparations for winter were underway. The days were spent busily pickling vegetables, preserving fruit and drying herbs, peas and beans for the cold months ahead. Strips of meat and fish were dried and packed in salt, and cheeses formed into large rounds and stowed away with the winter's store of flour and grain.

Alongside the provisions of food, Ma Howell was shoring up her store of dried wild garlic, ginger root, peppermint, thyme, barberry bark, coltsfoot, horehound, liquorice root and ivy for treating coughs and colds. On top of these were needed feverfew, for fever and headaches, mugwort, for purging the body, mallow, for aches and pains, plus lemon balm, lavender, witch hazel, fennel and raspberry leaves for soothing ailments both real and imagined which annually wracked the small community through the long dark months.

Kathren was proving a useful assistant and a keen learner.

She had not had the opportunity to learn herb-lore from her own mother, and Ma Howell took pleasure in teaching her grand-daughter and protégé about the properties of each herb and how they may be used to help or harm.

"Why do you not go to church Grandmother?" Kathren asked her one day as they were busy pickling roots and tubers for the winter store.

"Well I suppose I hardly see the point, the religion seems to me to change with the wind. I am happy to worship at home, in my own way. Be he a Papist or a Lutheran or a Calvinist, it's all one God to me." She shrugged and turned back to the pickling jar, into which she was carefully stacking turnips.

"Grandmother! I think that may be heresy!" Kathren smiled, "The Reverend Bradsell says you must go, that it's the law."

"I care as much for opinion of Reverend Bradsell as I do for this turnip my lass, less in fact! For the turnip has its uses and that fellow is..."

But Ma Howell didn't have a chance to tell her grand-daughter her opinion of Reverend Bradsell before there was a quick light rap on the door and small voice cried out "Please, come quick Ma – I've been sent to fetch you!"

Magret hurried to the door and opened it at once. Before her was a round-faced girl, aged about five or six, with dirty hands and a wide-eyed expression. "It's mother, she says to tell you it's her time and to please come if you can! Pa's out ploughin' and won't be back 'til dark."

The child was Mary Peke, whose mother Anne kept a small brewery on the edge of the village. This would be Anne's fifth labour, and all four of her girls had been safely delivered by Old Ma Howell. Anne Peke had been coming to Magret for morning sickness remedies and poultices for her aching back and joints for months, but she had also begged Magret for something to make sure that this time she bore a boy, as her husband was wanting a son to help with the farm work. Magret had given

Anne an old herbal remedy which her own mother had sworn by for getting boys. Anne was convinced that this pregnancy felt quite different from her others and was hopeful as the months passed and her belly swelled. But something was wrong. Anne should have been due after the new moon which was several weeks from now. It was too soon.

The birth chamber was shuttered and close, and Magret set Kathren to work building up the fire and strewing clean hay on the wooden floor while she threw soothing herbs into the flames and rubbed the groaning mother's hands and feet with a poultice. Ma knew at once that something was badly wrong – Anne was white as a sheet, limp and bleeding heavily, too much. Ma bellowed through to the anxious children clustered around the door "One of you, go for your father at once. I don't care if the fields rot, he must come now."

The baby came at last, small and weak and turned about the wrong way. He was too feeble to cry. Ma thought it unlikely he would last the night, poor little mite. His mother, too, was failing before her eyes. Anne's husband had come running through the village, arriving wild-eyed and filthy from the fields, asking for his wife, his child - how were they? What happened? What can he do? How can he help? Ma sent him for the Vicar, and the poor man returned with news that Francis Bradsell was gone to Winchester on business and was not expected home until late the following day.

The night drew on, and the baby's breathing grew more laboured. His mother's eyes grew dull and the smell of death permeated the rooms of the brewer and her husband. All of Ma Howell's skills and knowledge were powerless. Anne drifted in and out of consciousness until, an hour before dawn, her eyes snapped open and she called out softly for Magret.

Anne gripped Magret's hand, her flesh ice-cold and her skin grey and gleaming with sweat. "Please, Ma Howell, I beg of you, baptise him. I could not bear for his poor little soul to be damned. If he must die, let his soul return safely to heaven. If

91

there is no clergyman within twenty miles tonight, it must be you, or he will be condemned to purgatory for eternity."

Magret only hesitated a moment. Bradsell was gone, and while the church disapproved of midwives performing the holy rites of baptism, it was allowed in the most extreme circumstances. She took a basin of cool water and performed a simple blessing over it, then drew the sign of a cross on the baby's forehead and whispered a prayer over his tiny body. Anne gave a small sigh of relief. Moments later, she felt his small fluttering life flicker and disappear. She turned back to Anne and saw that she, too, was still.

Bradsell returned the next day, to find the village subdued and the family of Anne Peke in mourning. It did not take him long to discover the cause. His horror at the news was not lessened when he learned that old Ma Howell had performed a baptism on the child, and in his own village while his back was turned.

He railed against her to his servants, to the men he met in the village square, in the market place, to anyone who would listen.

"Of course the child did not live, no woman can mete out sacraments without consequences – it is unholy. More likely she opened the door a little wider for the devil to snatch the poor infant straight to hell."

"Likely the mystic herbs the woman was feeding to poor Mistress Peke is what fatally weakened her and the infant too. It is the devil's work, to interfere with the course of God's will. It is Vanity and it is Pride."

And so on, until most of the village had heard of Reverend Bradsell's anger with Old Ma Howell the Midwife.

That Sunday, Bradsell preached against the wickedness of women who presume to take the power of God and God's anointed servants into their own profane hands. His sermon brimmed with hell fire, his pale face alive with passionate fury. Kathren Kemp sat at the back of the church, her usual spot, ready to duck out in case she was called to attend on a patient with Magret. As Bradsell spoke, he glared at her over the heads of the gathered village as though he spoke directly to her and to her alone. She held his gaze as long as she dared before bowing her head, hands folded in her lap – she felt cold and sick. As the service came to an end Kathren rose quickly to leave but was prevented by a sudden grip on her shoulder. Reverend Bradsell was startlingly close to her, holding her tightly and looking down into her blue-green eyes with his own serious dark ones.

"I would speak with you, Kathren Kemp, if I may. Please wait, it is a matter of great importance."

The church was empty now and the last of the congregation were making their way down to lane towards their Sunday meal.

"Of course, Reverend" replied Kathren. She looked pointedly at his fingers still holding her tight and he snatched his hand away as if the touch had burned him.

"It is a delicate matter. Let me see – do you know of King James? Of Scotland?"

She was baffled. "No Reverend. I have heard his name spoken, but that is all."

"He is the heir to the throne of England, one day he will be King. King James is a great reformer and supporter of the purification of the church, and of her subjects. He takes a particular interest in the moral education of his people and is determined to stamp out un-Christian practices in his lands. You are a good Christian woman I think?

"I... hope so Reverend?"

"Then please, listen. Do not to follow your grandmother. Her time is over, the time of tolerance for such women is coming to an end. It must come to an end."

"Good sir, what do you mean by 'such women' exactly? Midwives? Surely the role of midwife is as respectable as any other?"

"I do not mean midwives, no… I think you know what I…"

"I'm afraid I do not sir."

"Do not make me foul my mouth with the word girl!"

"What word sir? I do not understand your meaning."

"Witches, madam, witches." He splutters in his frustration, "I believe your grandmother is a practiser of magic, a knower of forbidden knowledge and a heretic. She does not attend church, she has a store of knowledge of medicines and herbs that should be above her and she has presumed to the duty of a churchman in baptising an infant. I believe her guilty. And I mean to see her either recant and reform, or be punished as the Scots would punish her."

"Reverend, my grandmother is not a witch! She helps people, that is all, and if I can do the same, I mean to! Is it not Christian to help the sick and needy? Forgive me, I am only a girl, and not a learned church man like yourself. I am ignorant of scripture, but I have always believed that a Christian should help and heal when they can." She glared at him, her fists clenched tight at her sides, he did not seem to notice.

"There are methods of helping which damn the immortal soul while healing the earthly body, Kathren Kemp. I would not have you so endangered." He raised his hand and the tips of his fingers brushed her hot cheek, gentle as a kiss.

There was a moment of silence. Bradsell flushed and Kathren understood that she was in much greater danger than she first thought. She whispered a hasty "thank you" and something about getting home and slipped out of reach, out of the church, refusing to meet Bradsell's eye again.

Francis Bradsell stared at the spot on the cool stone flags where Kathren Kemp had stood a moment ago, where he had a good as declared himself to her with a word, a look, a touch. And she had run. For months he had struggled against his growing feelings, but the dreams of her were almost nightly now, confused and hot and waking him sweating and thirsty in the darkness. When he saw her in the village or at the back of his church on Sunday mornings, he was struck by a feeling of weakness that almost overcame him. He had, in private moments, imagined a day when the law would be passed allowing him to marry and he would be able to make her his wife, save her from her grandmother's wickedness, and make a Christian lady out of her. But she had run, and he felt the anger and shame swelling in his heart.

Old Ma Howell had a quiet winter. Few people came to her and she wondered at the silence of her kitchen and the empty lane. A child died of a fever but no-one came. Kathren had stopped attending church since the death of Anne Peke and her baby, so Magret's source of parish gossip was all but dried up through the dark winter. Instead, Kathren stayed at Ma Howell's side learning the skills of her trade. She learned to make a poppet, a good luck charm and a fertility spell for barren women, she learned to scry in a basin of spring water and read the phases of the moon and set a broken limb. She learned how to well-wish for the crops, for gentle weather, for travellers' luck and a fruitful marriage. At night Ma Howell took Kathren out into the garden and taught her to read the omens in the stars and where to pick mushrooms and certain herbs by moonlight in the nearby woods.

The new year crept in, grim and grey like an old dog, and still no-one visited Ma Howell's cottage on the edge of the village. When the first signs of spring appeared in the middle of March, Ma Howell learned at last why no-one had knocked on her door for a jug of warm ale all winter. Mary Swain was as swollen as a ripe berry, making her way from the church slowly past the lane and leaning on her husband's arm, when Magret came out to gather an armful of firewood from pile.

"Good day to you Kit, and to you Mary, and how are coming along my dear? I am surprised you have not asked for me yet. You look close to your time, and with this your first too… surely you would seek my advice?"

"Indeed Mistress Howell, I am very well and need no further advice, I thank you – my mother and aunt will serve me as midwives when my time comes, on the advice of Reverend Bradsell. You see I am well provisioned."

Magret bristled. "Indeed? Your good mother was certainly present at your own birth, but she has never delivered another woman's child, and your aunt is a spinster, is she not? And when, I ask you, has the holy Reverend Bradsell ever been known to deliver a child? To my knowledge the Vicar has never been within a dozen paces of a birth chamber and is no more a midwife than I am a Bishop. What is more, why do you address me now as Mistress Howell, when I have been Ma Howell to you for your whole life? Am I now a stranger?"

Kit Swain flushed a deep red, from anger or shame it was hard to tell, and Mary stared hard at the ground.

"Truly madam, I would not offend you for anything," she whispered to Ma Howell's feet "but Reverend Bradsell is our spiritual leader and a Godly man and he has forbidden us all from dealing with… with… you," she ended lamely.

The villagers in the road were stopping to watch and listen, some looked angry, others a little frightened. She turned on them too.

"And the rest of you, do you all fear me now? After three-score years of calling on my skills to care for your crops and animals, your wives and children, do you think me a devil now too?"

She did not wait for a reply, she whirled around and stormed back into her cottage, scattering small branches and dried leaves and slammed the heavy door behind her.

Early the next morning Magret and Kathren were woken by a heavy thumping on the cottage door, the sun was barely risen and Ma Howell wrapped a thick woollen shawl around her shoulders and went to the door.

"What is it?"

"Mistress Howell, we are here to arrest you in the name of the Queen. You are charged with the practice of malevolent witchcraft."

Ma Howell's eyes widened, then she laughed out loud.

"William? William Hawkins is it? And Nathan Gorney? And Richard Thorne is it there? What nonsense is this?"

William Hawkins, who had regularly stolen apples from Ma Howell's garden until the day he married and she presented him with a little sapling to plant in his own small plot, was deeply uncomfortable.

"Last night, Mary Swain lost her child – he was born dead and deformed at midnight. She claims you cursed her when she met you outside your house. There are witnesses who heard you call out to the devil when she refused your services. You are to be tried by ducking, Mistress. The Reverend has commissioned a stool to be built on the old bridge before the week is out. I'm sorry for it Ma, but you must come with us."

Over the course of the week that Ma Howell waited for trial, new accusations emerged, each wilder than the last. Thomas Peke's daughter Mary swore she heard Magret curse the fields as her mother lay dying. The Democks blamed witchcraft for the death of their cow and the Thwaites for their boy's broken leg, which had never healed quite right and had left him with a limp. Peke himself held Ma Howell accountable for the death of his wife, she was accused of poisoning poor Anne Peke with herbs disguised as cures so she could harvest the little boy's soul for the devil and prolong her own life. She was accused of casting love spells and punishing those of whom she was envious with sickness and ill-luck.

Francis Bradsell was in a fever of excitement. This day had been long in coming. He had sent for permission to build the ducking stool on Stony Bridge not long after the wretch Howell took it into her own hands to perform the baptism of the Peke infant. The plans were drawn and the carpenters and blacksmiths set to work building the holy instrument that would prove Old Ma Howell guilty.

How he hated her, and her beautiful grand-daughter, and their merry disregard for him and his church. At last, he would be rid of the witch, and his parish would no longer be troubled by rebellious women with blue-green eyes.

"Reverend Bradsell?" He looked up from his sermon. It was Kathren Kemp, her eyes were red and her skin blotched. Her hair and clothes were disordered and she looked like a wild thing blown in on the wind.

"Reverend Bradsell, I am come to beg. I beg you to have mercy on my grandmother, she has harmed no-one, she could harm no-one, and she is my only family. I beg you to take pity on her."

She fell to her knees, sobbing and he felt something like pity stir in him. He gripped it in his mind and snuffed it out.

"Your grandmother is to be subject to a fair trial, a legal trial. If she is not guilty, she has nothing to fear."

"Please sir, I have heard of these trials by water – the guilty live, only to be killed by fire or hanging, and the innocent drown. Innocent or guilty, it is death."

"The innocent are often saved before they drown, I have read."

Kathren sobbed loudly and Bradsell hardened his heart.

"Surely better to die a proven innocent than live accused?"

She looked at him then, anger in her eyes.

"It is my duty Kathren Kemp. I must not, cannot suffer a witch to live."

And with that, Kathren knew that her beloved grandmother was already dead.

On 23rd March, as the news of the Virgin Queen's death spread like wildfire across England, Kathren Kemp watched Old Ma Howell drowned, tied to a stool on Stony Bridge, in the same river she had lived beside her whole life. Deep in the folds of Kathren's clothing, a small wax figure bearing a graven cross on its chest began to melt against the warmth of her body. It was not a good luck poppet, or a fertility doll, and as she stared into the swirling water of the River Meon, she whispered a curse on the name of the man who had murdered Magret Howell.

1670 AD

The Wolf Woman

The Wolf Woman

John Hiett

The Honourable Edward Noel should have been a happy man. He was married to Elizabeth, eldest daughter of the Fourth Earl of Southampton. When the Earl died in 1667 Edward acquired the magnificent Place House and the Titchfield estates. They were blessed with a son, also Edward, who was born and baptised on the first day of 1669. He had servants and courtiers, and oxen and horses and goats; thousands of sheep grazed on his pastures.

Yet he was a worried man. Titchfield was in decline. No doubt about it. Only two years before, the vicar, Henry Tilley, had called a town meeting to discuss raising a tax for rebuilding the church tower, which was in a ruinous state. There was still no resolution to this problem. Half a century earlier the Third Earl had appointed Richard Talbot, surveyor of waterworks, to close off the estuary of Titchfield's river Meon. It was completed at great cost in 1611. The work allowed ships to reach Titchfield. The wool trade and other trades flourished, and the town prospered with it. But lately the river had silted up and was no longer navigable. Trade had fallen away, the population was reducing, and several notable families, including the Littlewoods on the High Street, had emigrated to the Americas. There were abandoned houses in the town, and his own rents were declining.

He had written to his brother-in-law, Richard, son of the Duke of Bedford. The Duke had completed the Bedford New River in 1651, guided by the Dutch engineer Cornelius Vermuyden. He was looking forward to Richard's visit. He would bring the Dutchman with him.

She was past her prime, but tall and lean still. Beneath her thick red hair her face was pale, but in that pallor two great eyes, their beauty enhanced by a dark veiled glow – and lips so fresh and ruddy they seemed to devour you alive. She had about her that look which is peculiar to women who are desperate to be loved.

They called her the Wolf Woman because she was never satisfied. The women of the town all made the sign of the cross when they saw her pass, with the skulking, prowling tread of a starving wolf.

Her father had been a foreman for Arthur Bloomfield at St. Margaret's Farm, who had seen her as a child helping her father. Her father died when she was 10 and left her an orphan. The overseer to the poor apprenticed her in husbandry to the Bloomfields, and she laboured in their fields.

At 21 she came out of her apprenticeship and married David Hawley. He was a good and faithful man. But at 23 she was a widow with a baby girl. She took over her husband's rented land, a quarter of a virgate.

She grew clover and hay, peas, beans, vetches and potatoes. When she harvested the potatoes she cut bracken and stored the potatoes under it to protect them from the frost. They lasted her until the spring.

She kept pigs and chickens and goats. The chickens were kept for their eggs until they were too old to lay, when they were killed and eaten. She slaughtered her own pigs. She was strong enough to lift the fat sow onto the bench and hold it down while she slit its throat. The small boys would come and watch, fascinated by the thick blood pouring out, and by the pig's squeals getting more and more quiet. They hoped for a trotter to take home.

She pulled it up on the tripod and with hot water and a razor cleared off the bristles. Then she would cut it up and salt the joints she wanted to keep for her own use. She would hang them from the rafters of her house.

Every part of the pig was used, from the snout to the curly tail. Parts she didn't want were sold in the Market Hall.

The sides of bacon were mostly fat, and streaky and salty. They tasted wonderful, and put some fat on her against the winter chills.

The little girl Mary was frail. "You'll never rear her" they said. But together they struggled through summers and winters until the new river came and changed their lives forever.

The great and the good of Titchfield were gathered in the Great Dining Room of Place House. The Honourable Edward Noel, his brother-in-law, Richard, the Dutchman, Cornelius Vermuyden, William Mayle, overseer of the poor, William Smith, Henry Lee, John Stokes, Arthur Bloomfield of St. Margarets, James Croucher, the woodheard, Thomas Oaken the tithing man and Henry Gaywood, gent. And there too was Thomas Corderoy, receiver for Edward Noel. He was already wealthy. He had lands in Abbotsworthy, Holborn in London and Beaulieu, all the gift of Thomas the Fourth Earl of Southampton, his kinsman.

The room held fourteen chairs covered with wool woven to look like Turkish carpets, and three stools in the same material. Six pieces of tapestry adorned the walls. The two large carpets were richly woven.

In the gallery above them was a clock and case and nearly fifty paintings, one of them a portrait of King Charles 1st.

Edward Noel called for attention. "We are here, Gentlemen, to secure the future of Titchfield. We are going to build a new river to the west of the Meon. Allow me to introduce my friend and kinsman Thomas Corderoy Esquire, who will be in charge of the building, and my engineer, Cornelius Vermuyden, who has a great deal of experience in building canals and rivers."

The Dutchman was standing at the long table. He had a leather bucket filled with sand and a large flask of water on the table. "My Lords, gentlemen", he said, "we are here to report on our plans. Already our surveyors have set out the line of a new river, from the mill to the sea-shore. We have dug trial pits. There are some variations, but we are mostly in clay."

"We will engage 16 gangmasters, and give each a furlong to dig. They will be paid by the yard, and each gang will be required to dig 10 yards a week. In this way we will complete the digging in 22 weeks."

"The finished river will be 20 feet wide and 6 feet deep."

"The river will be dug in two lifts in each section. One gang of men will dig to a depth of two feet and spread the material one foot deep on the sides. When that gang has advanced 10 yards the second gang will dig down another two feet. This will be nearly all clay. They will first throw the spoil onto the platform left by the first gang, and then onto the new river bank, making this bank another foot higher."

He stopped talking and emptied the bucket of sand onto the table. It formed a perfect cone shape. "You will see, gentlemen, that the sand is sloped at 45^0. That is the natural angle of lie, and that is the angle we must have for our new river sides."

He showed the gathering a drawing of the cross-section of the new river.

"The banks of the new river will be two feet higher than the surrounding land, and this will allow us to release water onto the water meadows when the new river is in flood."

Vermuyden stopped again, and poured water over the sand. The pile of sand collapsed into a sludge.

"You will see, gentlemen, that when a solid is saturated with water it acts like a liquid. We don't want the sides of this river to collapse. That is why, in addition to the sides of the river sloping at the natural angle of lie, the new river will be lined with clay from the workings."

Edward Noel completed the story.

"When the new river is working, cargo will be unloaded at the sea lock and transferred onto barges. These will be towed upstream on the rising tide and unloaded at the mill pool. Goods will be loaded there onto barges to return to the coast."

"This is a river, gentlemen, that will last for 100 years, and Titchfield will once again enjoy great prosperity."

It was evening. The Inn House in West Street was full of happy drinkers. Old Walter Churcher settled himself comfortably into the best chair and set off on one of his stories.

"I seed the owd king. I seed him twice. The first time when I was nobbut a young lad, no more'n 15 years or so. The king and his queen – Henrietta they called her. She were French and she had all they French ladies looking after her. The king, he was a fine looking man, with his thick dark hair and pointy whiskers and curly moustache. He had very thin fingers, as I recall. There was a lot of baggage and mules and horses, and litters for the ladies, and men-at-arms and a great crowd of attendants. Must have cost the young Earl up at Place House a lot of money to attend to them all."

"My Mum, who was in service there, said the king had brought a present for the Earl, six pieces of fine tapestry, more than 200 ells and five ells deep. They're still up there, covering the walls of the King's Room. Course we all went out to take a look and doff our caps. And they threw a few coins for us to scrabble for."

He took a sup of ale.

"The next time he came it was a cold day. It was November. He'd ridden down all the way from Hampton Court. That would be just before our Sophie was born. He came riding into South Street with only one man with him. Catcheside his name was. The king was weary. His hair and beard was grey. He had big pockets under his eyes. They'd been riding for five days."

"They rode to the merchant's house there at the end of the High Street. I ran to help him. He had a fine greyhound with him. Gypsy she was called, and a spaniel, Rogue. I put their horses in the stables at the back of the house, and rubbed them down with sweet hay. I gave them water and fodder. The two of them went into the house and sat by the hearth. Mistress Megan got them some broth and some wine. I could see that they wanted to linger there, but they had to move on."

"I don't know where they were headed for. When they came out I said to the King 'fine greyhound there master'. He smiled 'Greyhounds love their master as much as spaniels do, yet do not flatter them as much'. That's what he said to me 'don't flatter them as much.' Then they rode off, straight for Place House. Course that was where that Colonel Hammond and his troop were waiting for him."

"They was proper soldiers. Bright red uniforms, plumes on their helmets, shining leather saddles, shiny boots, jingling spurs. It was a fine sight."

"The colonel was very polite to him 'Sir' he said, 'I must beg you to come with me. We'll go across the water to Carisbrooke Castle. You will be safe there. I will care for you and attend to all your needs.' He bowed 'Your Majesty'."

"Off they trotted up Fisher's Hill. That was the last I saw of him. Lookee here. I've still got the little brooch he gave me for the small service I did for him."

"It was his last day as a free man"

They came from far and wide. From Stubbington, Swanwick, Burridge, Crofton, Feld Stoford, Lee Marks, Locks Heath, Fareham and Sarisbury. Hungry men, looking for work on the new river. Most walked from their own villages each day. There were many, too, from outside the parish who slept in the woods and the streets and were hard drinkers. The town was over-run by hundreds of men, many of them never chosen by the gang masters, but who returned daily in the hope of work. Most gang masters had their regular workers, but when one was short of workers he would blow a whistle and swarms of men would arrive looking for work.

One of these itinerants claimed to be of a Titchfield family in good standing – the Swains. He was a slow-witted man with eyes like rabbit droppings. No-one wanted to offer him lodgings, until the Wolf Woman saw him, and was immediately bewitched by him.

This was not the sweet young love that hesitates, that desires but does not ask, that promises but does not give. This was the searing love of a mature woman that devours with an urgency that forbids nothing. She wanted him at whatever cost.

She stayed close to him whenever she could, taking work where he worked. Her love was like a thirst in the hot hours of summer. But he did not notice her except to say "What is the matter with you?"

She followed him everywhere, "What is it you want?" he asked. "It is you that I want. That is all that I want".

"But I, Mistress, want your daughter" he said, "the heifer not the cow."

She fled, but soon slunk back. "Do you still want my daughter?" "What do you have to give her, to make it worth my while?"

"I will give her my house. It is enough for me if you will allow me a corner in the kitchen, and some straw to sleep on."

Her daughter Mary was unwilling. "Mum, I don't want to. Don't make me."

"If you don't take him I will kill you."

Thus they lived, she sleeping in the ashes of the hearth, Mary, not unwilling now, sharing the bed with Jack Swain. At every opportunity the Wolf Woman continued to make advances to him, and always he spurned her. "Get away from me" he would cry, "leave me alone."

"I'm not asking, I'm begging, Mr Bloomfield, let me work for you on the new river. You saw how hard I can work when I was your apprentice. I am as strong as any man."

Arthur Bloomfield hesitated. "I remember you well. But I can't afford to fall behind with the work. If I don't advance at least ten yards a week Thomas Corderoy will turn around another gang to work my section, and I will lose money."

"Just give me one day – half a day, please"

"Very well. You can start tomorrow morning. You will be on the bottom lift. It's all clay, so it's heavier than the top lift. That's the best I can offer you."

It was cruel, unrelenting labour. After rain those on the bottom lift had to clear the water that had collected before they could start cutting the clay. The Wolf Woman was as good as her word. She never stopped to rest. In the early morning melee she was always the first to be chosen.

There were not many men in the Inn House in West Street, but the biggest mouth was Jack Swain. He stood by the door. "Why should we be sweating our guts out, just to keep his Lordship in that big house? What has he ever done for us poor people?"

"You've only just come back to Titchfield, Jack Swain. The old Lord, Henry, he did a lot for the town. A lot of us worked at the new place, and were looked after very well. There was 24 bedrooms for the live-in servants."

"He started up the iron works to give us work. He built the market hall. He sorted out the wool trade so we could sell our fleeces."

"And his fleeces, don't forget his fleeces."

"And he paid for all that work at the estuary when he shut out the sea. My father worked there for a good spell. He had a decent living."

"And a few deaths," shouted Swain, "It wasn't all good. No, we'd have been better off if his family had never come here. It was my family made this town, not his."

Big Will Hoskins broke in. Will was typical of the rough spirit of Titchfield. No-one argued with Big Will. He was inclined to hit first and ask questions afterwards. He was always looking for trouble and not often given the opportunity to enjoy it. He said, patiently, "this new Lord, Master Noel, he's giving us work on the new river. If you was any sort of a man you would have got work there, but you're too lazy to stir yourself." "You think that's good for Titchfield? All those foreigners from Stubbington and Burridge and Crofton coming here taking our work and our women, fouling our streets, stealing from our fields. What's the good of that?"

Will Hoskins was getting angry. "You've got a lot of mouth, Jack Swain. What have you ever done for the town? You don't do any work, you live off other people's labour. That missus of yours is twice the man you are."

"She ain't my missus, and you mind your own business."

"You come here a stranger, saying you belong to the Swains. Did you come to old Thomas Swain's burial?"

"Yes, I did."

"I didn't see you there. When was he buried?"

"It was a few years ago now."

"No it wasn't. It was only a year ago last December. Have you called to see his widow?" Swain nodded.

"No you didn't. She died a month later, in January. I don't even believe you are a Swain. They was a good family. You are no good. You're just a rat. I'm going to call you that from now on. Jack Rat. I've seen you drinking from our ale jugs when you thought we weren't looking. And you've been messing with those young girls in the town. Isn't it enough for you to have two women in your house, you've got to bother little Elizabeth Finch?"

"I didn't go after her. She was the one that run after me."

"And why should she do that, a rat like you?"

"Maybe because I can give her more than you Titchfield men can."

"I think it is time you went along home, Jack Rat."

He didn't move and Big Will hit him straight in the face. Swain staggered to the wall, bleeding. He slid to the floor. No-one came to his aid.

"John Finch said he'd kill you for what you did to his Elizabeth. And if he doesn't kill you I will, if you come in here again with your thieving hands."

The Wolf Woman appeared in the doorway.

"Come on Jack, let me take you home."

He got to his feet. He had no friends, no job, no money, no respect. He saw in her the reason for his troubles. She was the woman who had invited him into her home. She was the one who had brought this upon him. He looked at her like a dog he was trying to lose. He hit her on the side of the head. She didn't flinch. She said, very quietly, "If you hit me again, Jack Swain, I will kill you."

Every time Jack Swain spurned her she would run off, looking down at her feet, her eyes black as coal. Still she came to him, again and again, and always he shouted at her, "Stay away from me, stay away."

Then came a hot August day. She was walking along the Ladies' Walk, from St Margaret's to Fernhill Farm, picking the early blackberries in a jug. She found Jack sleeping in a copse. She lay beside him. Her breath smelled of blackberries. Her body was soft and warmed by the sun. This time he didn't tell her to go. But afterwards he called "Stay away, leave me alone."

So it continued. She took him whenever she wanted him. And always he cried at her "Leave me alone."

Her daughter wept. She called her Mother a beast, a thief. She threatened her. "Do what you will" said her Mother.

Jack threatened her too. "If you come to me again", he said "as sure as God made little apples, I'll kill you like an animal."

"Kill me like an animal, for all I care" she said, "without you I have nothing to live for."

September is the sweetest month. The meadows are green, the harvest in. Blackberries and strawberries and mushrooms and slip-shell hazel nuts grew in profusion. The pigs fatten.

Mary lay on the river bank looking at the trout. It was still, facing upstream, it's tail moving just enough to stay in place against the current. Mary slipped her hand into the water and slowly moved it towards the trout's tail. She tickled it's belly with her fingers. The trout liked that. She slid her fingers towards the gills. It was a lazy, dreamy movement. When her hand reached the gills she moved her thumb and forefinger into the gills and closed her fist. She threw the trout onto the bank, where it thrashed about. She cut a twig in the shape of a Y and put one end through the gills to carry it home.

There were rabbits nibbling in the field. A stoat had caught one and was dragging it away. Mary took the rabbit off the stoat. It was still alive. She held it up by the ears and hit it on the back of the neck with a stick until it died.

She took it home and cleaned it and skinned it. The skin came off quite easily and she put it aside to cure. It would be part of a nice blanket for the winter.

The next morning she fell sick. She was hot and cold and shivering and trembling. Her mother knew that it was the summer sickness and that she would be dead by nightfall.

She gazed into the bright day, eyes wide open, the fear and fascination and wonder of death all around her. Death, near and inevitable and, like the wind, unseen, but there all the same. Poor Henry Tilley had died in August, leaving four young children, one a boy not yet a year old. The new vicar, Walter Garrett, was on his knees on the stone slabs of the aisle. "I'll come at once" he said. He had an affliction of the larynx. When he spoke he stretched out his neck like a crane, and his voice was deep and harsh. Even when he said something like "God be with you" it sounded like a curse.

At the house, already the bubo was in Mary's armpit, a painful, angry knob. It was a seething, terrible pain, with a pain in the head causing her to cry out in terror. Her groin began to swell with another bubo, and she was vomiting. He said to Mary, "Do not be afraid, child. You are blessed. The next time I see you, you will be in Heaven, where there is no pain, no hunger, only peace in the presence of the Lord." He spoke the comfortable words, but neither woman found any comfort in them. Then he prayed in Latin and left.

Later that afternoon Mary seemed to revive. She opened her eyes "Mum, I want to walk out and feel the sun."

"Jack" her mother called, "help me carry her outside."

"I will not. I will not touch her. She has the plague."

"You were lying with her last night. I heared you. Will you not help her one last time?" He walked away.

Wolf Woman lifted her gently, and carried her into the sunshine.

A mother hen shepherded her chicks. A sow wandered over to where one chick was stuck in a cow pat, and casually ate it. Children were laughing in the street. This terrible thing was happening yet nothing had changed in the world. The sun shone, the birds sang, the stream tinkled over the pebbles.

Mary turned her face towards her mother, a light of recognition in her eyes, like the brief flare of a match before it goes out, and she died.

Wolf Woman carried her into the house, washed her tenderly and sewed her into a woollen shroud. She lay her on her mattress and sat beside her through the night, filled with grief and disbelief and anger – anger at Jack, anger at God, anger at Mary!

In the morning she took her up and carried her to the churchyard. People watched her silently as she passed. Some doffed their caps. All alone she dug the grave and she alone watched as the Vicar conducted the burial. She filled the grave, gave the Vicar money for a mass. And the sun still shone and the

children still laughed. A life wiped out in one day.

Lady Penelope Daish was the same age as the Wolf Woman, but their lives could not have been more different. She lived in Place House, a friend and confidant of Lady Elizabeth Noel. She was childless. Her husband had been killed in the Civil War. She dressed modestly but elegantly. She was skilled at healing.

She was particularly keen on the use of honey. Place House had built-in bee boles from which a copious amount of honey was gathered. She knew that honey was the only food that did not decay. Indeed the Earls of Southampton and their families were pickled in honey in the vault below the monument in St Peter's Church.

She made potions and pastes from honey mixed with other ingredients to lay on wounds. She used sage and cloves and alum and vinegar and rosewater and onions. She gathered ivy and plantain, wallwort and elder, hawthorn berries, ladies mantle and marjoram and many others.

She was able to attend to the sick at Place House and often ventured into the town to help people there. She was the compassionate link between the town and the aristocracy.

Sleeping in perfumed sheets, eating good wholesome food in a sweet smelling dining room, she found the disease and smells of the town abhorrent. But she did not shrink from them. Like an angel of mercy she sought out the most wretched.

The old man lived in a ruined pigsty by the river. He was supposed to have done something dreadful in the Civil War. The little boys peed on him through the cracks in the walls, and lobbed stones onto him in his poor bed where he lay gasping for breath, with long hair, inflamed eyes and a tumour as big as his head on his arm.

She took him some linen, tried to clean his hovel. Sometimes she took him cake, and placed him in the sun on a bundle of hay. The poor old man, trembling and drooling, would thank her in his broken voice, and put out his hands towards her when she

left him.

It was a brilliant night. The stars in their thousands made the meadows as light as day. It was easy for Jack Swain to make his way to the old man's pigsty. He was shaking with a fever, holding a cross in his hands and mumbling a prayer through cracked lips. He hadn't noticed Jack Swain until he spoke. "I'll have that, old man." He took the cross. The old man wept. The growth on his arm was suppurating. Jack Swain poked at it curiously with the cross. He walked jauntily away and the old man scrabbled to follow him.

He wasn't the only one following Jack Swain. She, the Wolf Woman, rarely left him out of her sight. She hid in the shadows. When he reached the new river workings she confronted him, and upbraided him.

"Please come home with me Jack. Keep the cross if you must, but please let me take you home."

"Leave me alone. Get out of my way." He hit her and she fell to the ground. He kicked her in the stomach and screamed at her. "I told you I would kill you, and so I shall."

He began to drag her towards the edge of the workings.

The old man rose from the ground like a ghost. He struck out with his crutch. Jack Swain looked astonished. He stepped back and fell over the edge into the bottom of the workings.

She climbed down to him. He was lying quite still, eyes open. One hand was under his back, the other at his side, fingers curled as if trying to catch raindrops. There was a strange dignity about him in death that he had never shown in life.

"Stay here," she said to the old man, "I'll go and get help."

She ran to Will Hawkins and John Finch and told them what had happened. She begged them to help her hide the body.

They dug into the fresh earth of the towpath alongside the new river. It was easy work. When they had finished there was no sign of Jack Swain and no sign of any disturbance on the

new river bank.

Two days later the surveyor decided to put a sluice gate at that very spot, and the body was discovered.

The new vicar, Walter Garrett, a single man, decided to initiate the enquiry into the death of the vagrant. He called upon Arthur Bold, a lawyer and Member of Parliament, a Burgess of

Southampton and Portsmouth, Recorder of Portsmouth – and Manorial Court Official for all Titchfield courts.

He called together a court to decide if the four suspects in the death should be sent to Winchester Assizes for trial. He had Richard Norton, Justice of the Peace, Thomas Oaken, Tithingman for Titchfield, William Mayle, Overseer of the Poor and Churchwarden William Houghton, to help him.

The old man from the pigsty, the Wolf Woman, Will Hawkins and John Finch huddled in the Market Hall awaiting their fate.

The Vicar set the scene.

"We don't know the name of the man who died, but for the sake of this hearing we'll call him Jack Swain. We know that these four people buried him in the river workings. All four had a reason to kill him, and all four had the opportunity."

"He treated Mistress Hawley like a dog, and we know that more than once she threatened to kill him. He had got into a fight with Will Hawkins and both he and John Finch had threatened to kill him."

"The old man from the pigsty. We all know what sort of a man he is. We know what he did during the Civil War. We know that Jack Swain had stolen his cross."

"All four confessed to burying him in the new river workings."

Richard Norton, JP spoke. "It seems to me that they are guilty of concealing a death. But is there any evidence that one or more of them killed him? The old man is unable to speak for himself. Is there anyone here to speak for him?"

Lady Penelope Daish rose. "My Lord, I have some knowledge of these people and these events. May I speak?"

Richard Norton nodded assent. "Lady Daish"

"We know that Jack Swain was not his real name. He was a vagrant, a traveller. He pretended to be a Titchfield man so that he could live off the parish. He was lazy, dishonest and a thief."

"He was forever causing trouble in the Old Inn, stealing

other men's ale and starting fights. He treated Mistress Hawley like a chattel. He beat her and derided her for her love of him. He took her bed and lay with her daughter, while she slept amongst the ashes of the hearth. He despoiled young maidens in the town and cruelly left them to bear their shame. He stole from the old man in the pigsty."

"We have heard Mr Garrett speak against these four people. There is no evidence against any of them. There is every reason to suppose that none of them killed him. It may well have been a tragic accident. He was running from the pigsty and may have fallen into the workings and broke his neck. Let us look at these four people."

"Mistress Hawley had threatened him when he beat her. But she loved him with all her heart, and said she couldn't live without him. Now she has lost her daughter and the man she loved."

"Will Hawkins threatened to kill him 'if he came near him again'. But we know that he kept well away. It was said that John Finch threatened to kill him for violating his young daughter. But why would he have waited all this time? And the poor wretch from the pigsty. He hardly has the strength to walk, let alone kill a strong young man."

"No. We found a cross in Swain's pocket. It is that same cross which I gave to the old man."

"These four people together buried him in the workings. It may be that each thought that one of the others had killed him. They had all suffered from his evil ways. They are responsible for breaking the law by disposing of his body, but I beg your understanding."

"Our own William Shakespeare wrote ere long:
'The quality of mercy is not strain'd;
It droppeth as the gentle rain from
Heaven upon the place beneath
It is twice blest. It blesseth

him that gives and him that takes'

"So let us believe. Let us not condemn these poor people. Let us show them mercy. Let us decide that Jack Swain died of God's will, and set these people free."

Arthur Bold spoke. "We are here to administer the law. If one or more of these people were involved in the death of Jack Swain, they will go to the assizes and will surely hang."

The Wolf Woman stepped forward.

"My Lord. It was I who killed him. I had followed him that night. I saw him steal from that poor old man. I cursed him on the bank of the new river. He laughed at me. I hit him and he fell into the workings. I didn't mean to kill him, but I did. I know I will hang for him. It was I who persuaded the other three to help me bury him in the workings. I ask your mercy upon them, my Lords."

The court droned on about what would happen next. She barely heard them. She was thinking to herself "I've got you now, Jack Swain, or whatever your name was. You are mine forever. You and I are going to the same place. You will never escape from me there"

1891 AD

The Titchfield Tragedy

The Titchfield Tragedy

Shirley Bethell

Preface

It is a favourite ploy to take a true story and embroider it into a novel.

So it is in this case. The dates and most of the names in this story are true.

The author has dramatised the story of Alice Hinton, who murdered her children in 1891 in a house at the bottom of West Street, Titchfield.

Alice Sherlock was born in Swanage, Dorset, in 1855 to William Sherlock and Grace Wood. They had two sons, William and George, all born without the benefit of clergy.

Grace had been a milkmaid as a teenager, living in on the dairy farm with three other milkmaids and the dairy farmer and his wife.

She had to get up at 3am for the skimming, and by dawn was seated on her stool, forehead against the cow's warm flank, listening to the creamy milk squirting into the bucket below the udders. She hummed a little tune as she worked.

She was as happy in this position as she had ever been. She had simple pleasures. She would draw a giggle out of the other milkmaids by saying at bed-time. "I be as tired as Mrs Chivers, and you know how tired she were, don'ee?" (Mrs Chivers was known throughout Dorset because she had said, 50 years ago, "I be as tired as buggery".)

But as Grace grew bigger and stronger, so her hands hardened and the milchers became restless at her touch. When she developed a facial palsy the dairyman claimed that she turned the milk sour, and dismissed her.

By nature, Grace Wood veered towards the confrontational; she didn't like Welsh men on principle and had little time for Irish men, gypsies or Black men. She particularly didn't like prosperous folk on the grounds that they were undeserving.

Her husband, William, was the opposite. He was a happy soul. He had been heard to say that he had never met a man he didn't like. He had a nice sense of humour. He said that when he first met Grace Wood he didn't know whether to shake her hand or throw a saddle over her. Their two sons followed their dad in nature. Little Alice loved her father and her brothers, but was afraid of her mother.

Everybody was afraid of Grace Wood. She even frightened off her daughter's suitors, so that Alice got to the age of 20 without ever having a beau, and was afraid of being left on the shelf.

On the Whitsun walk that year she joined the other maidens. All were in long white dresses and carried a posy of flowers in one hand and a peeled hazel stick in the other. By the time they arrived at the green the fiddlers were already playing furiously. The girls danced with each other until the boys arrived after work, when there was some mingling going on.

Alice behaved completely out of character, and by the time she went home was no longer a maiden.

She didn't tell her mother until it became obvious what was amiss with her.

"Th' beest what?" Grace shouted. "You just bide here. I'll sort him out."

So off she set, hat clamped incongruously on her head, pinny tied tightly around her ample waist.

Jack Bettesworth was a dasher. At 24 he was enjoying life. Good looking, he worked for his father, a prosperous saddle and harness maker.

He was sitting at home that Saturday afternoon when he spotted, out of the window, Grace Wood storming up the hill, heavy umbrella in her fist, with Alice behind her weeping into her handkerchief.

Grace thundered on the door with her umbrella.

"Do Jack Bettesworth live her?" she asked his mother. "Upon my body and soul I have a big bone to pick with him."

"Th' beest this big man, bain't ee, with thy fine mistarshes and thy fancy hwome. Dostn't ee tell I 'twas not ee that ravaged my Alice's virgin innocence. Why be ee looking like ee doesn't get green malt on the floor? I tell ee, afore I go hwome we'll be setting the date of the wedding, as ee should have done five months ago."

Alice was weeping harder " But mother, I don't want to marry Jack. He is now already spoken for." Jack's mother spoke up. "This has come as a shock to us, Mrs Sherlock." (She called her Mrs Sherlock as a courtesy) "I would very much like to have a baby in the house again and bring it up comfortably as our own."

And so it was arranged. When the baby was born in 1878 it was christened Edith Bettesworth, and was taken into the Bettesworth household.

Alice stayed in her family home in the warm embrace of her brothers and parents. The brothers looked around for a suitable husband and found one in Thomas Hotson Jr. Thomas and Alice had a daughter, Augusta, in 1882, when Alice was 26, but within a year Thomas died of consumption, leaving her a widow with no means of support. She moved back in with her family. Augusta was a beautiful little girl with dark luminous eyes and a ready smile. Alice's heart ached. She wanted something better for her. She dreamed of meeting a tall handsome man who would sweep her off her feet and take her away to a fairytale land.

Most people can expect to get average luck throughout their lives. People say "He's lucky in business" or "He's lucky at games of chance" or "He's lucky in love." Others say you make your own luck, and that may be so. But if there is average luck it stands to reason that some are luckier than average, and some unluckier than average. Such a man was John Hinton. He was a good man, but bad luck followed him everywhere. He was so unlucky that people thought him a Jonah and avoided his company.

He lived in Swanage with his wife and two sons, William and Frederick. He earned a living as a collar maker. The two boys were mischievous little devils. She was driven to despair looking after them. So distracted was she by the boys that one day she scalded herself while taking boiling water from the fire to the washtub, and died. He was in a predicament. He was working from home, but the boys really needed a mother, and he didn't have much to offer. He wasn't tall and handsome. Nor was he prosperous. But he pursued Alice. He did all the running. Alice's thoughts were only for Augusta. Alice was in a very confused state. John wasn't an ardent lover, but he was persistent, and as Alice got to know him she came to see that he was a kindly man.

He was kind to his boys and he was kind to Augusta who liked him very much. Alice believed that she could come to love John Hinton, but she was afraid to leave the relative safety of her home.

Mrs Bettesworth, however, saw a chance to get Alice out of the life of her adopted daughter Edith. She spoke to John and offered to find him a house and a job in Chichester, where she had family, if he married Alice. That was the deciding factor for Alice, a new life in a new city with a new man. She thought his proverbial bad luck would have to change for the better.

dear missus Bettesworth
I don like to Ask you as you have been so Kind to us but it is not Working out as we Hoped for the children are been set upon cos of the way they Talk and little augusta has got a lisp chichester is Very Dear and john don make much Money as a colder maker is there any Way you can seeyourself able to help us out I hope littleEdith is Well and Growin up like a Lady Hoping this finds you as it Leaves me at present in the pink
alice Hinton

Dear Mrs Hinton

I am sorry to hear about your troubles. I have made some inquiries and I believe I can help you.

We have a friend in Titchfield, another harness maker, Mr Muckett. He can offer Mr Hinton a job, and there is a small cottage available to rent in the village. The rent is half a crown a week, and I have sent £1 to cover the first eight weeks' rent.

I will arrange for a carter to take you and your family and your furniture from Chichester to Titchfield. You will find that the people there speak very much like your children do.

Mrs Hinton, Edith is very well and happy living here with us. I don't want her happiness disturbed by any doubts about her parentage. You will understand that I am arranging this move for you on condition that you have no more to do with Edith, either by letters or visits.

I wish you all well, but this has to be the end of any contact between us.

Yours sincerely

Mrs Bettesworth

Augusta was quite frightened. The carthorse was struggling against the weight of the cart as they came down Fishers Hill, the driver lying hard on the brake. The two boys were standing up, showing off. John Hinton and Alice were glad their journey was nearly over.

Stony Bridge was bathed in sunshine, an omen, a welcome to Titchfield. They were looking forward to a fresh start.

They turned left along Mill Lane, leaving the Abbey and the Railway Hotel, and into East Street. There were a surprising number of public houses, the Wheatsheaf, the Crown, the Clarendon, the Queen's Head and the Bugle.

At the Bugle they alighted to run into their new home, a cottage on the corner of West Street and South Street. It wasn't much of a cottage. It had two bedrooms upstairs, a back kitchen and a front room. The tiled roof was in poor condition.

John and the boys unloaded their few sticks of furniture and carried them inside. Alice and Augusta set about doing the things that women do, making a home out of a house. She put her picture on the wall in the front room. It was in a gilt frame and showed an angel standing on what looked like a tomb, while four women looked up at the angel, and a beam of light shone downwards.

Titchfield was an attractive place. The streets were lit by gas from the new gas works in Bridge Street. There was a National School in West Street which cost only one penny per child per week. There was a lot of industry in the village, including the harness maker, Mr Muckett, who had offered John Hinton a job.

They had hardly moved in when they had their first visitor, the Vicar, the Rev Reginald White. Alice Hinton was quite flustered. "I'm very sorry, Vicar, I can't even offer you a cup of tea. I haven't got the fire lighted yet."

"That's quite alright, Mrs Hinton. I just wanted to welcome you all to Titchfield and to tell you about St Peter's Church and about the Sunday School."

When all was quiet Alice sat in the back kitchen, Augusta was asleep and John and the boys were out exploring. She began to weep. She longed to see Edith, her first child. The coming of the railways meant that a journey to Swanage was fairly easy. She could get there and back in a day, on the pretence of visiting her parents, and see Edith at the same time.

If only she could get a little bit of money she could take

a train from Fareham. But she had promised Mrs Bettesworth that she wouldn't go there again. She had lost Edith for ever. She sobbed bitterly into her pinny. She cried for her father, she cried for her brothers, she even cried for her rumbustious mother; and especially she cried for Edith. Already she had almost forgotten what she looked like.

Titchfield was an old established village with longstanding families. It wasn't easy for a newcomer to become accepted. The two boys settled in quite well, making friends in the school. Because the boys had lost their mother and Augusta her father, John and Alice treated them tenderly. There was no smacking and no scolding. The boys were little devils. William in particular was a rapscallion. He artfully used his temper to get his own way.

In South Street was a widow woman who earned a meagre living making chips. Customers brought their own bowl and for one farthing would get a bowl of chips. The widow woman supplied the salt and vinegar. It didn't matter what size bowl was brought, they all got the same amount of chips.

Whenever William could beg, borrow or steal a farthing he would grab a bowl and run into the chip shop. He wasn't prepared to wait his turn. He would run to the front, bang his bowl on the table, bang his head on the wall and generally upset people until he was served.

Their house was infested with black beetles. Every night the family had to take all the food out of the pantry and put it on the kitchen table, and take it back the next morning.

They could only afford a fire in the back kitchen. They burned coal, sticks, potato peelings, anything that would burn. In the winter evenings they would sit around the fireplace, the front of their legs mottled from the heat, their backs freezing. They made rag mats for the floor. Sacking was spread on the floor and old material cut into strips two inches long by half an inch wide. These pieces were threaded through the weave of the sacking, the two ends standing up on the top side. The boys were careless at this, putting any colours in any order and in an untidy pattern. Augusta's little fingers were much better, and she and her mother worked out pretty patterns for the finished rug. The boys were dismissed from the work. The rugs made the flag-stoned floor much warmer, and certainly prettier.

Apart from St Peter's Church there was a chapel in South Street run by Plymouth Brethren. They would hold public baptisms in the canal, to the derision of the rougher element in the village, of which there were many.

There was a working men's club and coffee room near the Bugle, and a Temperance Reading and Coffee Room on the corner of High Street and East Street.

In spite of these moral ornaments, Titchfield had the reputation of being a rough place. Alice never felt settled. She didn't seek friends. She kept herself to herself. She didn't seek help nor did she receive it, except from Doctor Hoare. He, kindly soul, felt a responsibility towards her and found an excuse to call in every week, and never took a penny from her in payment.

The Bugle Hotel was thriving. It had smoking concerts, for men only. In that hour of the evening when drunkards grew melancholy and wept for lost loves and lost opportunities, they would sing songs such as "Silver Moonlight", "Come like a beautiful dream", "Dream Faces" and "A Night with a Baby".

Sometimes a soloist would sing, and if he performed well enough the drinkers would throw a few coppers onto the performance area.

John Hinton had a nice tenor voice. His particular favourite song was Buttercup Joe. He would sing the verses and ask everyone to join in the chorus.

The M.C. introduced him. "Gentlemen, a new singer for us here in the Bugle, John Hinton. Best of order, thank you please."

Some unruly men would shout out different words of the verses to make them more bawdy, to great hilarity all around.

Buttercup Joe

I am a jolly sort of chap
My father comes from Fareham
My mother's got some more like I
and knows well how to rear 'em
Oh some they call I "bacon-face"
and others "Turnip Head"
But I can prove that I'm no flat
Although I'm country bred

Chorus
For I can guide a plough or milk a cow
Or I can reap or sow
I'm as fresh as a daisy as lives in the field
And they calls I "Buttercup Joe".

Those nobby swells they laugh and chaff
To see I eat fat bacon
They could not touch that country stuff
But that's where they're mistaken
On wine and grog they do their airs
And lord it at their ease
But I give I fat pork from the sty
Or a lump of bread and cheese
Chorus

Oh bain't it prime in summertime
When we go out hay making
The lasses they will all turn out
And freedom will be taken
They like to get us country chaps
of course, in harmless play
They like to get us country chaps
and roll us in the hay
Chorus

You should just see my young woman
They calls her our Mary
She works as busy as a bee
In farmer Kellyson's dairy
Oh bain't her suet dumplings good
By jove I means to try 'em
And ask her if she wouldn't splice
With a rusty chap like I am
Chorus

It was the spring of 1891. The first green buds were on the trees. The people of Titchfield were shaking off their winter listlessness, getting excited about the new life springing up all around them, feeling the sun, saying "good morning" to one another, it was a time of hope, a feeling that good things were about to happen.

But not for Mr Muckett. There were two other harness makers in the village, and he was finding it hard to keep his head above water.

He called John Hinton into the room behind his shop. "I'm very sorry John, but I can't afford to employ you any longer. I can pay you until the end of this week, but I'm afraid you will have to find another job. You are a good worker, and I will give you a good reference."

There was plenty of industry in the village, but jobs tended to go to Titchfield people, not newcomers. John set about looking for work straight away, but there was nothing available. While he was still looking he tried to earn a living selling winkles he picked up on the beach at Hill Head.

Alice felt the weight of the world on her shoulders. She picked flowers to sell – cowslips, bluebells, primroses in tiny bunches, sweet smelling violets. In the summer holidays the boys helped as much as they could. They picked dandelions, until Alice told them "they make you pee the bed". At the end of summer they picked mushrooms in a field past the Abbey. The boys even drank milk direct from the cow's udders, until they were into calf and taken into the laying-in shed.

When it came time to go back to school after the summer, there wasn't enough money to pay the penny a week for all of them. John Hinton said "We'll send just Augusta. Boys can earn a living without education, but children learn at their mother's knee, so it is more important to educate girls than to educate boys."

Alice was getting increasingly confused. When John came home one day she said distractedly "I can't find Edith. Where can she be?" "Edith is well, Alice, she's living with Mrs Bettesworth in Swanage."

On another day she said to him "Who are you? What are you doing in my house? Go away or I'll ask my Thomas to throw you out."

The children were really hungry. They begged scraps from neighbours. They were often out on the streets in the cold. There was no money for coal. They were burning skirting boards from the house.

The final straw came when the truant officer called. "You must send your children to school Mrs Hinton. It is against the law to keep them at home. You can be fined if you don't obey the law."

Alice didn't know which way to turn. She couldn't afford to pay for the schooling and she couldn't pay a fine. Could they take her children away from her? She couldn't bear to be parted again from a daughter. Augusta was only nine. She still had a lisp. She still had big round eyes, more often than not now filled with tears. But the children's lives with her promised only hopelessness. That very week they had eaten nothing but boiled bran.

She became quite serene as a plan formed in her head.

She told Doctor Hoare that her wedding anniversary was on November 15. (it wasn't)

The good doctor, knowing that she had nothing in the house sent, at his own expense, a chicken, some vegetables, a fruit pudding, a bag of coal and kindling and some candles, so that they could have a celebratory dinner that evening.

Alice cleaned the house, put on her Sunday dress, put Sunday clothes on the children and told them all it was a party for magic.

After they had eaten their fill, for the first time in months, Alice told the children that they could each have a wish, and if they wished hard enough it would come true.

John was bewildered by the whole performance, but he was anxious to avoid hurting Alice, and joined in the game.

Alice said, "my darling Augusta, you are my youngest, and you shall have the first wish. You can wish for anything in the world. What would you like?"

"Oh Mummy, I would really like to grow up as beautiful and kind as you are. And because I will be beautiful and kind I will marry a rich man, and have lots of children to sit on your lap. And we'll have parties and plenty of coal. That is what I wish for."

"And you, William, what is your wish tonight?"

"I wish to be a soldier, and wear a fine uniform and a sword. And I will keep you safe."

"And Frederick, my big boy, what do you wish for?"

"I wish to be a farmer Mummy. I will live in a big house, and keep sheep and cattle, and chickens and pigs. And I will grow corn and potatoes, and we will never be hungry again. And you and Daddy will come and live with me, and you will have no more worries."

The children were excited. "Will it all come true, Mummy? Will it happen as you say?"

"I promise you, my sweet lovely children, all your troubles

are over. Go to bed. Have sweet dreams. Look forward to tomorrow."

She put them in one bed and covered them with a coverlet of pink patchwork squares.

November 16 1891

The screams coming from the Hinton house that morning brought people running in through the unlocked door. Augusta's piercing child's voice was heard across half the village, begging for help. John Fielder and Tom Swain were the first in, followed by Dr Hoare and P.C. Harfield. They found a scene of horror. The children were bleeding to death, and Alice trying to kill herself. It took four or five men to restrain her. "Let me be. Let me go to my children. I can't live without them."

Dr Hoare bound up her wounds, and P.C. Harfield took her to Fareham, where she appeared before the magistrates at 12 noon that same day.

On the advice of Dr Hoare they committed her to Knowle asylum to await trial at Winchester.

Alice Hinton stood in the dock in Winchester Assizes on March 29 1892, Alice had spent four months at Knowle Asylum. It is not known what treatment she had there; it may have been electric shock treatment. In any case, Alice was very subdued in the dock. Her eyes were frightened and she uttered not a word. She had been examined by a doctor to determine whether she was fit to stand trial, whether she could understand the charges, whether she was able to instruct a lawyer. The doctor ruled that she was insane.

There were very few witnesses – P.C. William Harfield, some neighbours, Dr Hoare and her husband, who had not been present at the time of the killing.

In his summing up the judge instructed the jury "You are not here to determine Mrs Hinton's state of mind. You are here to decide the facts. Did she or did she not kill one or more of the children, as charged."

The jury returned a guilty verdict after a short retirement.

The judge told her counsel "Mrs Hinton has been found guilty of killing her children. But she has also been declared insane. I will make an order to commit her to Broadmoor Criminal Lunatic Asylum in Berkshire."

Alice Hinton remained in Broadmoor until her death in 1945. Near the end she said that she never had one completely happy day for the rest of her life.

A poem was written by David Blake, as follows

LINES ON THE TITCHFIELD TRAGEDY

On the 16th of November , in the year of 1891
In the little town of Titchfield, a murderous deed was done,
By a woman Alice Hinton, to call her by her name,
She killed three little children, who never were to blame.

It was on a Monday morning, the sun did brightly shine,
When these three little children, were by their mother slain,
Policeman William Harfield, entered by the door,
And saw the daughter Augusta, laid lifeless on the floor.

That noble policeman, he did his duty well,
The sight he saw that morning, no other tongue can tell,
He rushed in through the kitchen, caught Alice by her side,
For if he had not done so, by her own hand she would have died.

The doctors soon attended, and worked with will and skill,
They did all in their power, to save poor little Will,

But all they did that morning, their labour was in vain,
For soon poor little Willie, was numbered with the slain.
The doctors in attendance, were Oliver and Hoare,
They did all in their power, as I have said before,
They came to Alice Hinton, her wound they neatly bound,
It took five able-bodied men, to hold her to the ground.

A cab then was ordered, to take her right away,
She was brought before the magistrates, at 12 o'clock that
day,
The doctor then came forward, and said she was insane,
She was sent to Knowle Asylum, and there she was detained.

These three poor little children, that ne'er did any harm,
Were called away to Jesus, who took them in his arms,
Their souls have gone to Heaven, their bodies to the clay,
And all who lived in Titchfield, will ne'er forget that day.

Two months in Knowle Asylum, Alice Hinton did abide,
She was brought again to Fareham and before a Justice tried,
She was sent to take her trial, at Winton County Hall,
Charged with wilfully murdering, her three poor children
small.

Yes, on the 29th March, in the year 1892
The murderous Alice Hinton, again was brought in view.
Before the Judge and Jury, she appeared in the dock,
The case came on for hearing, at exactly 2 o'clock.

The people and the jury, and likewise Justice Day,
All gave the best attention, to what there was to say,
The Jury found her "Guilty", that the children she had slain,
But on the doctor's evidence, it was proved she was insane.

There is a partial gravestone in St Peter's churchyard. It reads:

Erected by the children and others of Titchfield in memory of
Frederick Hinton
aged 12 years
William Charles Hinton
aged 10 years
Augusta Ho ----
aged 9 ---
who died -----
God will wipe -----(the tears from?)
Their eyes ----
Death -----
Neither ----

John Hinton emigrated to America to join the gold rush. At immigration desk on Ellis Island the official mis-spelled his name, and his papers read "John Hilton". The change of name brought a dramatic change of luck. As an old man, while living in his hotel in New York, he reflected that, by and large, his luck over the whole of his life had been average.

1943 AD

Love Letters

Love Letters

Lorraine Davies

(an Epistolary novel)

Prologue

Mervyn Ebenezer Davies was born on 23rd August 1919. At the age of 15 he joined the Royal Navy. His service record describes him as an errand boy. When he reached man's estate he was a quarter of an inch short of 5ft 4 inches, with a chest measurement of 35inches. He became a telegraphist in November 1937 and was serving when war broke out in 1939.

In the early part of the war, after the French signed an armistice with Germany, most of the French fleet was in the Mediterranean, controlled by the Vichy (unoccupied France) government. In 1941 part of the French fleet was in harbour at Marsel Kadir in northern Algeria. A Royal Navy squadron demanded that the French ships be demilitarised, in order that the Germans could not use them. The French refused, and the Royal Navy attacked, sinking one capital ship and damaging five more. Over 1200 French sailors were killed. Some of the French ships escaped to Toulon, where the French navy was.

Mervyn Davies joined the K class destroyer Kandahar in the Mediterranean on December 26 1940. The destroyer hit a mine on December 19 1941 and was irreparably damaged, with the loss of 73 out of a complement of 183 officers and men. Mervyn was awarded the Distinguished Service Medal for that action.

In 1942 Admiral Auphen, who was the Vichy Secretary of the French Navy, ordered the scuttling of the whole fleet in Toulon, to stop the Germans using them. 72 vessels were sunk, including 25 capital ships. The few remaining French warships, in other waters, were controlled by the Free French Navy.

Mervyn volunteered for submarines and joined HM S/M Usurper as a petty officer telegraphist.

On June 8 1943 Usurper left Holy Lock for its second war patrol, heading for Gibraltar and Algiers. She arrived in Algiers on July 11.

From July 14 he wrote 27 love letters to his wife Lucy. All began with the same salutation and all ended with the same blessing. All filled an airmail letter. The first and last letters are published here in full, with excerpts from other letters.

"I don't wanna say goodbye for the Summer,
Knowing the love we'll miss.
I'll send you all my love ev'ry day in a letter,
Sealed with a kiss"
by Peter Udell and Gary Geld

HM S/M Usurper

14.7.43

My dear Darling Wife and Sweetheart

I'm sorry I haven't written for the last two days, but you'd never believe how busy I've been this time. I've been very lucky. A chap I knew before has been sent down to help me, and he's a trump. Anyway, I've managed to do everything I've been wanting to do. Still, why talk of work when there's love on board. Yes, love, because it doesn't make any difference how far apart we are, our love will always bridge it. Whatever else we may have to sacrifice during the war, that is one thing nobody can ever take away from us. I love you more than all the world, my Dear, & I want you to know that I shall always be the same. We have had no more mail yet, but I've read those letters that I had the other day more times than I'd like to count. You don't know how happy they made me. They are just now playing Deep Purple on the radio, & it makes me think of you so much. That song is more than just a song to me. It's a symbol of all that I hold most sacred, our love, the happy days that we spent together, and those that we are going to spend soon.

I do love that photo too. You look so dainty & neat, and so happy too, yet with it you combine that saucy little hat. Result, I get a perfect picture of my favourite wife. Thank you Darling. I know that it's not easy to get photos now, but I can tell you this, you can't possibly send me too many. I've got them all stowed away, & each one is my favourite – I love them all. That poem too, I think it is beautiful. I've read it so often I almost know it off by heart, and I still love it as much as when I first read it. All these things are sweet & beautiful to me because they remind me of you, in fact, they're part of you. I've had a couple of nights of real homesickness just lately, Dearest, I have missed you so much & I want to come back to you & never leave you again, but as the poem says, there's a job to be done first.

Still, once that's done, we'll settle down & build that little home we've dreamed about.

They'll be happy days, getting our things together bit by bit, & each piece will be a new treasure, a symbol of all we've hoped & worked for. Isn't it funny, our children will never realise what each piece of furniture means to us until they are grown up. Several bits of Mother's furniture that I used to think ugly, must have been really beautiful to her.

You know, when I turn in at nights, I think of you & wonder if you are thinking of me, tho' I suppose you are. I don't get very much time during the day, especially just lately, but as soon as I turn in, I come straight back home. I have some wonderful times too, I wouldn't miss my dreams for anything Lucy, I can't possibly tell you all you mean to me. I should have to be a poet or a master musician to do that, but I can prove it to myself just, & then to you, by the way I live, & my constancy to our love. Believe me, Dearest, I shall always be true to you.

I hope you have a good time on your holidays & I'm glad that Gladys is able to come with you. Give her my very best and, of course, to all our friends at home. What is Doreen's son's name?

Don't forget, Sweetheart, I'm yours body and soul, now and always. God bless you, my love, and watch over you.

With all my love
Your adoring husband
Mervyn xxxxxxx
Love from Percy to Betty

HM S/M Usurper
15 July 43

What lovely memories we have. That walk through the woods with Maud and Arthur was lovely dear. You make a lovely picture underneath the trees. I'll never forget that time we went down to Christchurch, just before we got married. I bought you a cup of tea in the morning & that was the first time I'd ever seen you in bed.

Everything here is going on fine, my tummy gave me a bit of the usual trouble the other day, but thank goodness, it soon went away again. Percy, John & I went sunbathing this afternoon, without costumes. Poor old Percy caught the sun a bit, I bet you'd have laughed.

Today is our carnation day, Darling. This time last year we were together & three years before that, I met you for the first time. This year there are no carnations, but I'm still thinking of you sweetheart.

8th July 1943

My Dearest Darling Mervyn

I hope you are still receiving my letters and that you are well. I too love getting your letters — it's almost like you are here beside me when I read them. I hate being parted from you my Darling, as I miss and love you so very much.

I am not quite sure how to tell you this, but I think I might be expecting. I have been to the Dr, but he's unable to confirm it yet as it is too early, but from the way I've been feeling I think I am. I really can't believe it, and I was so worried that if I told you, you might be cross with me; or are you pleased? I can't wait to hear what you think.

The village is very busy. There are Yanks at Hollam House. The kids go up there and ask "Got any gum, chum?" and come back with chocolate and cigarettes. Some of the young girls in the village come back with nylon stockings. It looks like silk, but is artificial. I don't go, of course. I wouldn't do that. But they do look very nice on the legs. The Yanks get them from their PX. I don't know what PX stands for. Could it be part exchange? In any case, old Mrs Roberts got a pair of nylons. She won't wear them. She's keeping them for her funeral. She's going to go to her maker wearing nylon stockings.

There are more soldiers in tent lines on Meon Road. They keep our village bobby, Mr Lockyear up on South-ampton Hill very busy.

Miss Parry, who rattles around all alone in St Margaret's Priory, runs the WVS. I asked Miss Parry if I could join the WVS, but she turned me down. I don't know why. They have a very smart green uniform.

Lady Chalmers, wife of Admiral Chalmers, runs the services canteen. A lot of the soldiers like to go there. I saw that Ralph Richardson go in last week. He parks his motorbike outside Madge Cousin's house.

HM S/M Usurper
16 July 43

I've had three air letters from you today, Dearest & I'm the happiest man alive. I've been ashore for three hours, but I came aboard early so that I could write to you. You said that you didn't know whether I should be cross or proud to be a daddy. Lucy, my own, if we are lucky enough to be really starting a family, my chest will be so big I won't be able to turn in my bunk.

I see by your letter you've already seen the doctor about it, you will let me know as soon as you know anything, won't you dear. I won't say that I'm not worried, that would be a lie, but I'm as happy as I can be.

I am so sorry to hear you've been on the club, and that you've had to put off that weekend at Christchurch.

We have some wonderful memories. When things don't look so good, I always try to remember some of our happier days, and that always makes me feel happier.

Lucy thought she should do her bit for the war effort by volunteering to work in the services canteen. When Lucy went into the canteen she found two young officers at a table. One was in army uniform, one navy. They were speaking in French. She had never heard French before. She was enchanted.

The navy officer was Jacques Fuguet. He had decided not to live under the Nazi jackboot in Paris, and came to England to join De Gaulle's force. He was in the Free French Navy.

The army officer was Lt. Richard West. He looked no more than a boy. Before the war he worked in the theatre. At Dunkirk he was told to march on south with his platoon. He spoke French very well, and the French people were generous with food and drink. He was told "Every man for himself".

At Saint Nazaire there was a troop ship in the harbour, with 2000 men on board awaiting evacuation. He was refused permission to board. He slept that night in an abandoned ambulance. In the morning he watched as German dive bombers sank the troop ship, killing all on board. He hitched a ride on a trawler in the harbour. Back in England he was seconded to General de Gaulle's forces as a liaison officer.

He was stationed in Portsmouth, and had heard about the Shakespeare connection in Titchfield. On a whim he had borrowed a staff car and brought Jacques Fuguet to Titchfield.

Lucy hovered around the two young men, fascinated. Richard said to her "Miss, do you think you could find us a cup of tea?" Jacques said to her; in English, "Young lady, could you spare us a little time to tell us about your village?" His English was even more entrancing than his French.

Lady Chalmers bustled in and tried to take her away, but Jacques said to her "Madame, I would consider it a great courtesy if you would allow this young lady to talk to us for a little while". Who could resist his Gallic charm?

Richard watched while the conversation continued between Lucy and Jacques. A line of a Rupert Brook poem came into his mind "I dreamt I was in love again, with the one before the last". He mused, how our lives are changed by a whim.

Jacques was wearing a ring on one finger. It had an odd shaped cross on it, with two horizontal bars. "It is the Cross of Lorraine" he said. "It is a symbol of French Patriotism and of a Free France. It is on the flags of all Free French warships".

By the time they left to go back to Portsmouth Jacques and Lucy had agreed to meet again at the dance in the Drill Hall on the Saturday.

He was an accomplished dancer. The band was more enthusiastic than talented. They danced the quickstep and the waltz, but she especially enjoyed the slow foxtrot.

At the end of the evening he asked if he could walk her home. Dusk was falling. They walked through the village. There was a soft breeze, and she shivered. "Are you cold, Cherie?" he asked. "No, I'm not cold, I just had a feeling that I will never see you again".

"I hope that is not so. I have to go away tomorrow. I can't tell you where. But whatever happens, when this awful war is over I will come back to Titchfield. I would like to give you my Cross of Lorraine ring for you to remember me by". The ring was too big for any of her fingers, but she kept it in her jewel box for the rest of her life.

HM S/M Usurper

18 July 1943

This is just a short note to tell you that everything is alright & that you are not to worry about anything. I was working late last night & so didn't get a chance to write, but I know you will forgive me. I had a snag on one of my aerials & whilst I was working on it, I put my wrist out. It is as bad as it was before. I haven't seen anyone about it yet, but if it gets any worse, I will, so don't worry.

Darling, I can't tell you how eagerly I'm waiting for a letter to tell me for certain if I'm going to be a Daddy or not. I do hope so. You said you can't understand it, but I don't know. I don't profess to know very much about these things, but I should imagine it is quite possible. It looks as if it must be. Fancy me coming home and having a wee son (or daughter, I don't mind) all of my own. It doesn't seem possible, does it? Don't forget, Sweetheart, I shall want a bulletin with each letter, or I shall get worried.

HM S/M Usurper (Lt. D.R.O. Mott DSM,RN) had her first war patrol in the Norwegian Sea in April 1943.

On July 18 1943 she departed Algiers for her second war patrol. She was ordered to patrol to the west of Corsica.

On July 27 the Usurper torpedoed and sank the French Chateau Yqem about six nautical miles south west of Ajaccio, Corsica. Chateau Yqem was in convoy with Cap Corse and escorted by the Italian torpedo boat Orsa and the German auxiliary submarine chaser U3 2210. The U3 2210 ran up the torpedo tracks and dropped depth charges and believed the submarine was sunk. To make sure, two escort vessels hunted the submarine throughout the night. At 19.07 hrs Orsa got an echo but then lost it. At 19.25 hrs contact was regained, and Orsa dropped twice four depth charges, followed by two more and observed air bubbles and some oil. But HMS Usurper had escaped.

The next morning they searched again, without result.

At 16.45 hrs Usurper sighted a convoy of two merchant vessels, fired two torpedoes, and then went deep. The escorting destroyer dropped ten depth charges without effect, then was in contact with Asdic. Eleven depth charges were dropped. Usurper finally surfaced at 0028/28 and cleared the area at speed.

On July 28 she attacked the Cap Corse with four torpedoes. No hits were obtained. At 20.05 hrs she returned to periscope depth and sighted a liner of about 4000 tons at a range of 8000 yards. She fired four torpedoes with no hits.

Usurper returned to Algiers on August 4. She had developed a serious fuel leak which kept her out of action for some time.

HM S/M Usurper
3.8.43

I'm anxious to find out if I'm going to be a Papa or not. I'm not feeling too bad at all now. I'm still a bit shaky really. I've had ten days turned in this trip. I don't know what was the matter, but when everybody else was wandering about in pants only, I was turned in with an extra blanket and a hot water bottle. A couple of days in the sun will soon put it right.

I've been thinking of you so much, & wishing I could write to you, or at least let you know that everything was alright. There are lots of things I would like to tell you, but they wouldn't let me.

The Captain was awfully good to me while I was rough. He used to come along every day to see how I was getting on, & then I got up one day for a couple of hours & made myself worse. After that he forbade me to get up until about two days ago.

6th August 1943
My Dearest Darling Mervyn

I received a letter from you today telling me that you have been poorly for ten days, and I am beside myself with worry. It should be me looking after you, my love, but this blessed war has torn so many people's worlds apart. I would give anything just to see you again, even if it were for just a day. I love and miss you so very much and it breaks my heart to know that I can't be with you and have no idea when we will be together again.

Last week I saw young Paul Cousins playing with his toy submarine. It is powered by an elastic band and he had it going in their tin bath. He was dropping marbles on it. He said they were depth charges. My poor heart nearly broke. But the little lad meant no harm.

He's got a lovely voice. He is senior boy in the Church's Boys choir. There are 24 of them, and they won first prize at Bournemouth Choir Festival the other week.

HM S/M Usurper
6/8

Thank you very much for the lovely letter I got today. It is wonderful to keep getting them & also to know that you are getting mine. I'm afraid to say that I went ashore yesterday for a walk and came over very bad. So now I'm turned in the sick bay of our depot ship. Don't worry, there is nothing very much wrong, the doctor boils everything down to my old trouble. I hope to be back on the Usurper again in a few days.

You asked me if I could remember 15th July four years ago. Of course I can, Sweetheart. That was the day when I fell in love with you. I've never regretted that love. Now, when we look like being parents, it is the most important thing in my life.

P.S. You win Dearest, my beard is gingery, tho' how you could have guessed, I'm dashed if I know.

HM S/M Usurper
7/8/43

There is something else that I'm very interested in hearing, and that is the doctor's verdict about the other matter. I shall be really worried about it until I know definitely & if it is true, I expect I shall be even more worried. As long as I hurry up & get out of sick bay & back to my boat, I have high hopes of being with you by that time, tho' of course I'm not counting on it. Don't worry I reckon I'll be out again by tomorrow.

I may have a couple of days at a rest camp. It will be a good change anyway. I've had less than two full days away from the boat so far, but I feel better for it. Another chap, a friend of mine, is looking out for the boat, so I've got no worries in that direction.

HM S/M Usurper
8.8
You know, in some of my previous letters I've been rather selfish. I've been saying how pleased I am that we might be going to have a baby, without thinking of your point of view. I know that you too want a baby, but you wanted to wait until I could be home with you. Believe me, Lucy Dear, if it comes true, tho' I can't be with you actually I shall never leave you for a minute in thought. It's a terrible thing to have to bear it all alone, without anyone to be with you and comfort you. Oh Darling, I know I've been blind, but you must forgive me. Our love has been so perfect, so full, now this has happened to crown it.

I hope your holidays are as perfect as you've been wanting them to be, and I hope you got a good few sessions in (Don't forget that photo' in the costume.)

HM S/M Usurper
12.8

I've just had two days in a rest camp. I went straight up there from the sick bay, and I had a really good time, swimming and sunbathing for a couple of days. I feel good and fit again now.

By the way, Lucy Dearest, if it is true, are you going into a nursing home for it? I leave that entirely up to you. I'm only a mere man, and it's nothing to do with me. Not much, just wait till I get home.

Do you remember that night in Dunoon when we were lying together, & you told me all your most secret dreams? I think that was one of the sweetest times we ever spent together. If it is humanly possible I'm going to make all those dreams of yours come true.

P.S. I believe I'm allowed to tell you now that we have had a success one trip

1st August 1943

My Dearest Darling Mervyn

I was hoping to get a letter from you today, but no luck. The days seem to be dragging by and I wish with all my heart we had some idea when we are likely to be together again. Just for you to be able to hold me close to you & tell me that you love me as much as I love you would be wonderful; I keep thinking of that memorable time we had on Dunoon.

I have some news for you (promise not to laugh) but I thought I should do something to help the war effort and I have got a job as an electrician — even though I don't know how to change a plug! I'm sure I will soon learn & it will be nice to be with other people as well.

It costs me four pence return to go to Fareham. Sometimes the bus conductor doesn't charge me, but I have to pay 3 pence for the single fare home so it doesn't save me much.

I went to the Parish Rooms on Saturday to see the Sunshine Kids. They are tap dancers. They are ever so good. I don't know where they are from.

The Church also puts on magic lantern shows there for the children. It's mostly pictures sent back by missionaries showing black people in Africa. I suppose if you are ever patrolling in the Africa area you'd be too far away to see them.

HM S/M Usurper
13.8

I was hoping for a letter today, but there was no mail. I can tell you, Darling, I'm really anxious to get my mail now as soon as possible.

I'm sure you had a really good time on holiday, and hope that work isn't too much of a drag after it. Gladys is a very good friend to go on holiday with, I should imagine, really good sport.

You know, there are so many things I want to say about the other thing, things that I feel I ought to say, and yet I just don't know how to start. It is so difficult to put things on paper. If I could only hold you in my arms for a while I could say everything so well. Even so, Dearest, I felt that you understand. You always have understood me.

August 6th

My Dearest Darling Mervyn

I've still not heard for definite from the doctor, but Flo Churcher dangled my wedding ring on a piece of string over my tummy, and said that according to the way it turned I was going to have a baby girl. Isn't that nice?

If you see anything nice for the baby where you are, would you get it for her?

I don't know why, but I worry about you now even more than I have in the past. You've been at war now for nearly four years, and maybe it's because the end of the war is in sight I get more anxious.

I think I am going to give up that job as an electrician. I'm not enjoying it, and sometimes of a morning I feel quite sick and I just don't want to get on that bus.

HM S/M Usurper
16/8

You spoke as if our baby is now a certainty.

I'll try to concentrate on getting home in time to be with you. I love you so much that I can't bear to think of you being on your own. Thank God you are with Millie, she really is one of the very best.

You mentioned leaving work, which is something else that makes it sound definite and I agree with you that it is best for you to leave as soon as you can.

Darling, don't worry about me. We have a family motto "Davo's are never downed", and nothing is going to happen to me. I'll be home again just as soon as I get the chance, and if I could, Sweetheart, I would never leave you.

I will look out for something nice for the baby; I'm afraid I'm going to be very unlucky, but you can trust me to keep my eyes open.

8th August

My Dearest Darling Mervyn

I do hope that by the time you receive this letter you will be on the road to recovery. I have been so worried about you, my love, especially knowing there was nothing I could do but wait for your next letter, which, as yet, has not arrived.

I don't know if you have given any thought to a name for our baby, but how do you feel about either Michael or Anthony if it's a boy, & either Laura, Jane or Elizabeth for a girl?

I went to Bognor with some of the girls from work yesterday and we all had a good time. At least it lifted our spirits & the weather was fine. All I could think of was you & wished I could be with you to look after you.

I go down to Arthur Hales' shop every week to recharge the wireless battery. He charges me sixpence a time. Every week I complain to him that the battery doesn't last a week, and every week he tells me that I'm using the wireless too much. But there's some lovely programmes to listen to, as well as catch up on the news. I especially like Variety Band box on Saturday evening, after my bath. I hope you are thinking about me on Saturday evening!

I try to imagine, when I hear the news, what you may be doing. There's so many boys from Titchfield who won't be coming back.

HM S/M Usurper
17/8

Thanks very much for the mail I got today, a letter, two County Press and the book of Coastal Command. By the way, Dear, that magazine you got was arranged by me. It makes me so happy to get a letter from you, you always seem to have something marvellous to say.

When you said you were going to Bognor on holiday, I thought you were going near the beach, but I do envy you your country holiday. We must do the same thing ourselves when I come home again..

You asked me if I could think of any nice names for baby, well, I think I like the ones you suggested very much.

I should have loved to come out mushrooming with all of you that morning, not only because I'm very fond of mushrooms fried, but also because in the early morning & out in the fields with the right company, is a pleasure that wants some beating.

HM S/M Usurper
19/8

I wasn't able to write last night, but believe me, it wasn't my fault. I was very busy, & I look like being even busier for a while. Don't worry, tho' Darling, I'll write at least every other night.

Now about that arm, It's quite ok now, Lucy,

166

I can't think of any job I used to do that I can't do now. I can carry any weight, Dear, so please don't worry. I can't tell you how happy I am about everything, & I say a little prayer for you every night you know.

I love you with all my heart and soul. I shall always belong to you, my Darling. My heart is at home now & all I want is to come home and find it again.

HM S/M Usurper
23/8

There's just one thing, Dearest. You said in one of your letters that you had had a really bad turn. If you still haven't seen a doctor yet, do please. Or even Nurse Gardner. You don't know how worried I am, after all, you are everything I've got, I should be absolutely lost without you.

You said you weren't so thrilled as some of your friends seem to be, but just wait until we are in each other's arms, and talking about the wee'un (wain to we Scots), you'll be really thrilled then.

I used to think I belonged to the Navy, body and soul, & maybe I did, but then I met you. Meeting you changed my whole life, made it fuller, happier, and certainly much more human.

23 August 1943

My Dearest Darling Mervyn

Today has been a very happy one for me, as I received 2 wonderful letters from you. I have read them over and over again. I, too, miss you so very much and love you with all my heart. Also, today is your birthday and I do hope you have received my card in time. How I wish I could be with you to say "Happy Birthday" in person & give you a birthday kiss (or more!) but, I hope, as every day goes by it is one nearer to when we will be together again.

I will be seeing the Dr soon & I hope he will confirm that I am definitely expecting. From my point of view, I am pretty sure I am. Thank goodness Mille and Alfie will be here for me when the time comes. I don't know what I'd do without them.

Mr Spurway the vicar was preaching last Sunday and talking about our boys who are away fighting. He said "They've got something we men at home never have. They are lions. It's better to have one day as a lion than a lifetime as a mouse".

That's you, Darling, a lion. I'm ever so proud of you. It must sometimes be frightening, though you never admit it. But when you are frightened, remember that I love you dearly and I'm proud of you.

HM S/M Usurper
26/8

Thank you very much for those birthday cards I got today, & believe me, they made me very happy. They're as welcome as the flowers in May.

I'm waiting now for the letter that tells me definitely that I'm soon to be a Daddy. I'm as excited as it's possible for anybody to be, and I know that I shall love it almost as much as I love you. I don't think I could ever love anybody like I love you, you are my first and only love. I think when children come the parents' hearts must get larger to make room for the extra love they bring with them.

I'm glad to hear that Doreen's baby is getting on so well, & looks so lovely. I'm getting very interested in the subject of babies now. I went ashore the other day and saw some baby clothes in a shop. I would have bought some, but I can't for the same reason as you can't get all you would like. If I do get a chance to get anything that will be useful, I will, of course.

HM S/M Usurper
3.9

I'm very sorry I haven't written for a couple of days, but I've been to the rest camp for 48 hours, & I've had a really good time. Swimming, sun bathing and just lying about reading. I enjoyed every minute of it. Last night was best tho, I didn't have one drink (a record). I went for a walk along the beach. You were very close to me then, my love. There really is something about stars that make me feel romantic.

I'm longing to hold you in my arms again. The way the news is going, it might not be very long before we get our happiness again. That's the day I'm living for.

HM S/M Usurper
4.9

My love for you is the strongest feeling in my life, & I can say this truthfully, I wouldn't have it any other way for all the world. I want with all my heart to make you happy & to make you as proud of me as I am of you. I defy any man to feel happier or prouder than I do when I walk arm in arm with you down the street. Now this news that you are going to have a baby has made a difference. My love has become gentler, more tender.

I'm glad you enjoyed that dance at the drill hall the other night, only I wish I could have been there with you.

By the way, my love, have you seen the Doctor yet? I get so worried about you after all, you're just everything to me, Dearest.

HM S/M Usurper
6/9

It's a lovely day today, my Love. I've had another two letters and I can't possibly tell you how
happy they make me. More than that, I got a pho-
tograph & I think you must be getting more beautiful
than ever. I like your hairdo, Lucy, tho' I'm afraid
if I was home I should mess it up.

By the way, you know I had ten shillings in the
bank ever since we were last together. Well, I'm glad
to say I've managed to put another five pounds in.
I'm going to try and save hard from now on. I don't
go ashore here, only when I go to rest camp.

So you were really thrilled when Doreen's baby
smiled at you. I think you're going to be the lovingest,
loveliest, charmingest mother that ever was.

As for that pint that Doreen's father wants to
have with me, tell him I'd give five bob for a pint of
real English beer. We can't get that here, English
beer.

HM S/M Usurper
7/9/43

Your letters have bucked me up immensely. I love
you so much, Darling, that your letters make all the
difference between a good day and a bad day to me,
even tho' I know it's not your fault when I don't get
one. You know, when we think of the time our letters
used to take just after we were married (remember?)

I reckon we're really lucky now. The average time seems to be about a fortnight, and that's pretty good, really, isn't it?

I don't suppose we shall know how long we are likely to be out here until we actually come home again, but I've got my fingers crossed. I think if we get home about the middle of February that will be just swell. Who knows, while there is life there is hope, and if I've got very little else, I've got plenty of that.

HM S/M Usurper
8th Sept.

This is a great day, my love, isn't it?

Now that Italy has packed up they've taken months, perhaps even years, off this war. Now that one of our three main enemies is OUT of the war, maybe soon I shall be able to devote all my time to making your dreams come true.

How I wish I could have been in England tonight. It must have been a wonderful evening.

I'm longing to hold you in my arms again, and feel your lips pressed on mine.

Oh Lucy, I'm just living for the day when you and I can settle down in that little home of ours. We dreamed about it and hoped for it so long that it really must come true.

My whole heart is yours Darling, and my whole life is devoted to trying to make you happy.

Aug 30 1943

My Dearest Darling Mervyn

I do enjoy reading your lovely letters. I keep them all safely so that our grandchildren can enjoy them in the future.

I had a spot of bother, but it's over now. The War Office stopped some of my allowances. Some superannuated generals sitting in a cosy office in Cheltenham have the job of saving the government money. They do this by stopping the allowances of the wives of servicemen. Madge Cousins arranged for me to see the vicar, Frank Spurway, and he sorted it out for me. I lost a couple of weeks' allowance, so those generals have earned their corn.

You really suffered to earn your D.S.M. and no doubt those generals will get a medal for making me suffer.

That Mr Spurway is a lovely man. Do you know he played cricket for Somerset? He was a wicketkeeper.

His two girls, Odine and Fenella are really blossoming now. Lovely girls.

But he's getting a hard time from the three Hewett sisters who live in Bridge House. They have their own pew in Church (as do Lady Chalmers and Miss Parry and the Fielders). But the Hewitt sisters know the Bishop, and they make Mr Spurway's life a misery.

On that cheerful note I'll close now.

Your ever-loving wife,

Lucy

HM S/M Usurper
9th September

Many thanks for a really lovely letter I got just
this evening. It really is wonderful what a difference your letters make to me. I read every word of
them over and over again, they always bring me a
new thrill, a few moments of pleasure in a day that
is pretty full, just lately. The radio is just playing
'Warsaw Concerto' & I always feel that I can write
better when I'm listening to a drop of good music.
    You're my guiding star, & I try to live as much as
possible as I know you would have me do.
    By the way, Dearest, if you are for sure going to
have a baby, you really mustn't worry or fret about
me at all. You really mustn't for BABY'S sake. I've
got my fingers crossed hoping to be with you before
(she?) is born.

HM S/M Usurper
11/9/43

That last letter came out very fast, my Dear, it
only took six days, so that I got it on the actual night
of your party. I was thinking of you last night and
wishing you a very happy time.
    I have some news for you too Lucy. Do you re-
member the T.I. Bent? Well, Mrs T.I. is going to be a
mother at the end of February, and she was told she
couldn't without an operation. Just think, in a mess

174

of four, two of us are going to be Daddy's at the same time. All I'm waiting for now is the letter confirming it, and I'm going to have it included in the news.

Just think, too, there is a chance I may be home before then. We'll be really happy then. Oh Lucy, my Sweetheart, I long to be back home with you again, you mean Heaven and earth to me. I can't imagine what life would be without you.

HM S/M Usurper
Sept 13th

You asked me how the girls out here like my beard. Well, as far as I can remember, I've only spoken to one girl, and that was in a café when I was at the rest camp. I'd like to have you see the place. It is set well back from a road running through a wood & it's very pleasant going out in the cool of the evening under the trees, with a bottle of wine at your elbow. By the way, the girl I spoke to was working there, and the conversation consisted mainly of me asking 'How much' and being told.

While I was ashore yesterday I meant to have a photo done. I beg your pardon, I meant a picture. It's almost impossible to get a photo here, but you can get a pencil drawing for about five bob. But the chap who does them was outside his shop working on the pavement. I didn't fancy sitting out there so I still haven't got a picture.

HM S/M Usurper
14th Sept.

If we can only get this bit of the war over, we may
have a little time together before we start somewhere
else. I'm always thinking of you and wondering how
you are getting on. I'm very anxious about you now,
my Dear, and keep on wishing I could be home to
look after you. That sounds silly, me looking after
you, but I should know that everything was O.K.
right up to the minute.

Look, Sweetheart, if you ever want to contact me
very urgently for a special reason, you can get a
special form from the Commodore R.N.B. Portsmouth
for an extra quick telegram. An ordinary telegram
would take longer than these air mail letters. I hope
you don't need one until next March.

Do you remember that poem I sent you? Well the
words of that poem express my love for you far more
than I can possibly do myself. I just know the ordinary words.

8ᵗʰ September

My Dearest Darling Mervyn

I am so excited about writing to you today as, at long last, Dr Windemer has confirmed we are expecting our first baby — you are indeed going to be a Daddy towards the end of February! Everyone is thrilled for us here and, whilst I am hoping and praying you will be here for the birth, I know I am in good hands with Millie and Alfie to look after me. Millie and I took our Leslie and Sandra to the fair yesterday. Sandra got straight on one of the horses of the carousel and enjoyed every minute of it, while Leslie didn't like it a bit and refused to get on! I hope, when this terrible war is over we will be able to take our baby to the fair together & I know you'd need no persuading to sit on a ride. Isn't that a wonderful thought, my Dear?

That Paula Rogers is a mischievous little scamp. Her family goes to the chapel, and Paula went there early last Sunday with that Pam Price, and they played the organ, Paula pumping, Pam Price on the keys. They had locked the door and even the minister couldn't get in!

177

HM S/M Usurper
19/9/43

I want to thank you very much for a lovely letter I got today. The mails haven't been very good lately, and I've been hoping for a letter for some time now. You can imagine how welcome it was.

I'm surprised Leslie didn't like the fair, I used to be mad on them when I was just a kid, and you can take it from me that I'm not too old now.

I'm glad you managed to get Sandra to laugh when she was on the horses. I know what a wonderful way you have with children, and with grown-ups too, if it comes to that.

I haven't written for three days. I've had a fit of the blues and I was afraid if I did write my letter wouldn't be as nice as you deserve. One thing Lucy, your letter snapped me out of the blues alright, and I'm feeling happier now.

HM S/M Usurper
27/9/43

Oh Lucy we shall never be very rich but our baby will have something that lots of really rich people don't & that's pure unselfish love. I'm praying that I shall be with you when our baby arrives. I'd give all I own to be with you right now.

I'm sorry that Gladys can't go to Roy just yet, but for your sake I'm glad because I like Gladys and I think she's a really good friend.

It's one of the things I've noticed how your friends and their families make me so welcome. They are all so friendly and homely even tho' they never met me ~~before~~.

I didn't tell you that SPO made me a writing case did I? It's quite a nice one with the word MIZPAH on the inside and a sailing ship on the outside.

HM S/M Usurper
c/o GPO London
23/9/43

My own darling Wife and Sweetheart

Once more I'm trying to think of something new to say, but if I can't think of anything now I shall still go on saying the old things. If I don't manage to write you'll know why, won't you Dear? I want you to know that I love you with all my heart and soul. You mean all the world to me, my sun and my star. In the words of the poem I love you to the level of every day's most quiet need, by sun and candle-light. I love you truly as they turn from praise. I couldn't say it better if I tried. ~~Even though I can't~~ say it in my own words, I want you to know that these are truly sincere. We've had some wonderful times together haven't we Sweetheart. Bristol, Swindon, Falmouth, London, Newcastle, Scotland; that place

will always have a wonderful attraction for me now-
adays. I first met you there, I first courted you there
and I first asked you to be my wife there. You know
Dear one, we've got something now that will live for
as long as either one of us is still alive. The joy of
true love, freely reciprocated, and the memory of true
happiness all over England. No matter where we've
been together we've always had a wonderful time,
and you have always been a really perfect wife and
partner. That's how I want it to go on, Sweetheart.
Always together, no more of these hideous partings
and worrying (on both sides) as to whether the other
is alright. I want to come out of this war safe, in one
piece, to be able to come back to you, a proper man.
Do you remember what I once said to you when we
were courting, about being able to look after you and
do my best for you? Well I still feel that way. I want
our baby to have the very best of everything too.

I can still remember having to go to school hungry, and one morning I couldn't get off my knees
after morning prayers & had to be carried out. That
is never going to happen to OUR baby, Lucy, not
while I'm alive. I'll work my fingers to the bone if
necessary. This is getting rather forbidding, isn't
it? I do feel rather strongly about these things tho'.

I hope everything is going alright at home and
that the sickness you told me about isn't so bad. It
must be rotten for you, home there, I wish to goodness I could come to you before February. Never-
mind, perhaps I will. I've got my fingers crossed

and keep you in my prayers. Remember me to all at home, and maybe ~~before~~ too long I'll be able to do it myself. I'm looking forward to getting this parcel very much. I want to see those photographs. I think you get lovelier all the time, Lucy. I know that to me you are the loveliest girl in the world. That isn't all though. You are the sweetest and most charming girl in the world, and there aren't very many lovely girls who have both those virtues. When I think of some of our sweetest moments I think I must be the luckiest chap alive. In Bournemouth, when I brought your morning tea, and your face was just in sight, I can't tell you how lovely you looked but you were (as you always are) really beautiful. In Scotland, when you told me all your hopes and dreams. When you said goodbye to me early one morning in Plymouth. There are dozens of them, pearls stored in my heart, helping to make this parting tolerable. I shall have to pack up now, but I want to tell you that you have always been a wonderful inspiration to me and always will be. God bless you Sweetheart, and bring us together again soon.

With all my love, your adoring husband Mervyn.
MIZPAH xxxxxxxx

On September 24 HMS Usurper departed Algiers for her third war patrol. She was ordered to patrol off La Spezia. Late on October 3 she was ordered to move to the Gulf of Genoa. No further contact was made and she failed to return to Algiers on 12 October as expected. The German anti-submarine vessel U3 2208 reported attacking a submarine in the Gulf of Genoa on the morning of 4 October with 69 depth charges in six runs.

It is often believed this may have been the Usurper. However, the most likely cause of HMS Usurper's loss is due to mining.

The telegram to say that Mervyn was missing, presumed dead, arrived on the same day as Mervyn's last letter.

Epilogue

Lucy's daughter was born on February 22 1944. She named her Lorraine. She remarried in 1949 and had two more daughters, Valerie and Carole.

HM S/M Usurper was discovered off the coast of Tunisia in 2018.

Jacques Fuguet survived the war and returned to live in Paris. He never came back to Titchfield.

Richard West fought through Italy. When he reached Milan he was asked to put on a show for the troops. He took over a theatre, dressed some ballerinas in feathers and sequins and had Alfred Marks coming on in top hat and tails singing "In days of old a glimpse of stocking was always considered shocking but now who knows, anything goes".

After the war he followed a career as a director in rep, and retired to live in Menton, in the South of France. He died there in 2017.

I thank Paul Cousins for his remarkable memories of Titchfield in 1943.

1950 AD

Vanishing Vandals

Vanquishing Vandals

Margaret Pace

It was a chilly Saturday night in March that the clocks were to be put forward an hour to British Summertime. Mick, the Verger, lay sleepless in his warm bed in the cottage near to St Peter's Church. Through his mind wandered the problems of the day as be tossed and turned. So many jobs to do and the list never got smaller. The tiles on the floor of the chancel were needing attention, he was afraid that someone would trip if he didn't fix them soon. Then the area behind the organ was getting cluttered up with music stands and boards, and easels. Everyone was using the narrow space to put their useful 'not to be thrown away' junk in there and the vicar had asked him again, only this morning, if he could sort it out.

Mick tossed and turned. There was another problem that was worrying him, too, the vandalism that seemed to be getting worse. What could he do to stop those youngsters damaging the church? Already that month the young hooligans had pulled down the outside notice board and smashed the tower lighting. It was a real problem.

Thinking of tomorrow's Sunday services, Mick suddenly remembered that he hadn't altered the church boiler clock to

185

switch on the heating, that had to come on by 6.30 am or the church would be freezing for the 8 o'clock service. How stupid of him not to remember it before. Ah, well, he consoled himself, no harm done, at least he could do something about it now. He pulled on his heavy grey woolen dressing gown over his pyjamas, grabbed a torch, and headed out of the house, absentmindedly tucking his balaclava into his pocket. He found he needed that more and more these days, working in, and around, the church in all weathers.

Grabbing his torch, he set off through the churchyard to the Vestry door. Unlocking it, he went over to the key cupboard and selected the large iron key to the boiler house. Locking the door carefully behind him, he walked quickly round to the front of the church to the boiler house. There were steps down and it was almost under one of the box tombs near the large stained-glass window, next to the belfry tower.

Mick fiddled around for some time with the boiler controls, cursing that his torch battery was on the blink. Finally, he was finished. He was turning to leave when he heard voices nearby. He listened, young voices, a nervous giggle, a suppressed laugh.

"Go on Ron, try and hit that figure half way up the window. Bet you can't, you plonker." A different voice chimed in, "He's lost 'is bottle."

"No, I aint, I gotta find the right size stone."

"Come on, then, get a move on, we can't hang about all night. What about the cross at the top, I bet you couldn't hit that, you weedy oik."

Mick felt a surge of elation pass through him. At last he could catch the boys in the act of doing something, "I'll show them, the vandals," he thought, "I'll really put the fear of God into them." He quickly pulled his balaclava over his head and eased himself out of the boiler house shutting the door slowly behind him., the hinges protesting eerily, as he knew they would, because he hadn't got around to oiling them. That was one of

186

the jobs on his 'to do' list.

He made a dreadful moaning cough and held the flickering torch under his chin. Still groaning, he slowly walked up the six steps. It must have seemed to the boys, standing nearby, that there was a body coming out of the tomb. They scattered with yelps of sheer terror.

"That'll teach them a lesson." thought Mick, grinning, He made sure they were out of sight, running as fast as they could up the road, before he made his way back to the Vestry to return the key inside the church.

Mick was a grown man. He didn't believe in ghosts, but when he was a child, with a child's vivid imagination, he hadn't been so sure. His elder brother had told him of a ghost in the church and reminded him of all those dead bodies in the churchyard, mostly good people but some dreadful ones, too.

His brother told him that there was a witch who had been burnt at the stake, 400 years before and whose restless spirit was said to roam those ancient walls, crying silently to be buried in holy ground. The witch was waiting for the right combination of a full moon and a naughty child to be able to show herself.

Mick smiled to himself, that's what brothers did, frighten their siblings. As he turned away from the key cupboard, Mick glanced down the chancel to the Southampton Chapel. An eerie glow shone around the effigy lying on the ornate tomb. As Mick stared, a figure seemed to take shape, a wispy, floaty image of a bearded man, wearing a fitted jacket and stockings with a white ruff round his neck. He seemed to look directly at Mick with a half-smile on his deathly pale face. He clapped his hands together slowly and silently, three times and then dissolved back into the tomb.

Mick rubbed his eyes, had he actually seen the Earl of Southampton's ghost or was it a trick of the light? He couldn't have imagined that silent clapping, could he? It was almost as if the friendly ghost had enjoyed Mick's own ghostly performance

187

outside the church. Well, well, well! Mick chuckled, praise really, when you remember that the Earl of Southampton was Will Shakespeare's patron, and, in his lifetime, must have seen a great many important plays performed by the best actors of the day. I've missed my vocation, thought Mick, as he made his way home. I wonder what the Vicar will say when I tell him about it tomorrow.

The Authors

Taliesin Driver hides his/her identity behind a nom de plume, but knows Titchfield well.

Lois Bird won a BA in Ancient History from the University of Leicester, and followed this with a Master's in Classical Mediterranean. She lives in London and works in the Events and Marketing industry, with the aim of opening her own marketing company. From this she will be able to combine her passion for history and her events experience to advertise and fundraise for museums across the country.

Margaret Thompson is a Scot, has lived in Titchfield for 36 years with her husband and three children, but is still considered an incomer to the village. She is a retired doctor but continues to carry out some academic research.

Peter Hiett has been a journalist all his working life. After graduating from Oxford he worked on local newspapers in Cornwall and Glasgow before becoming a stringer for the BBC in Jakarta and Tunis, at the same time writing for national newspapers. He has worked for the BBC in London for 28 years. He is very familiar with Titchfield and has written for the Titchfield News.

Margaret Pace retired to Titchfield 25 years ago. She joined Word Wrights writing group in 2000. She has had several poems published and has been a regular contributor of stories, articles, poems and reviews to the Titchfield News. She initiated and coordinated the "Eyewitness Acount" book, published in 2007. She is now writing her "Life and Times" for her future great grandchildren.

Rosa Johnson is a well established Titchfield author. She has written two children's novels and one novel for adults. She has also written a pantomime (the Willow Platter) and as a member of the Titchfield Arts Community Theatre both acted (with her husband David) and wrote sketches for the show. Rosa continues to write poetry and short stories.

Hannah Hiett studied English Literature, Drama, Classical Mythology, Art History and Creative Writing at Manchester University. She is fascinated by the representation of rebel women in history, literature and folklore, and plans on smashing the patriarchy one witch tale at a time. She lives and works in Newcastle Upon Tyne but is a life long visitor to Titchfield.

John Hiett, a mining engineer turned marketing man, has lived in Titchfield since 1981. He has been chairman of the Bowling Club, Treasurer of the Allotment Society and secretary of the Millennium Committee. He was a founder member of the Friends of St. Peter's, is a member of TACT, the History Society, the Bowling Club and of Stubbington U3A. He sings in the U3A mixed choir (tenor) and in the Hampshire Police Male Voice Choir (baritone). He lives a full and happy life in a community he loves.

Shirley Bethell was living in Epsom when she began to know and love Titchfield through friends who lived there. She honed her story telling skills on her five children and 13 grandchildren. She now lives blissfully in a house overlooking Swansea Bay and close to the Gower Peninsula.

Lorraine Davies is the maiden name of Lorraine Finch, daughter of Mervyn Davies RN, DSM. Lorraine lives in Peel Common and knows Titchfield well. She was unaware of her father's letters until her mother died five years ago, when she found them, tied with a blue ribbon, together with his service record.